Sculpting Amanda

Julie Sanford

Sculpting Amanda

Nobody is born a victim, but they can be made one.

Meet Amanda Wake, starting her new job. Her only requirement is to earn enough money to buy a coveted mobile phone. Seventeen and fresh from school, she dreams of a Mills and Boon love story developing between her and her new boss.

Meet Mathew Mason, A successful businessman, and Amanda's new employer.

What Amanda doesn't know is that Mathew has aspirations too. He has an unhealthy and immoral obsession with Amanda.

The job was created so that he could have better access to her. Set over the course of sixteen years we follow their journey.

Amanda's life is plagued with many unfortunate twists and turns unbeknownst to her all due to Mathew's intervention.

A dark and disturbing suspense thriller that will have the reader screaming out for a book buddy just so they can discuss the plot. Not for the faint hearted, read sculpting Amanda if you dare.

This book is entirely a work of fiction, none of the characters are based upon anyone. (Which is good, because they would have had a terrible life!)

This book contains disturbing scenes and is prohibited for anyone under 18 years old.

Finally, I hope you enjoy reading this book as much as I enjoyed writing it.

I felt I had no choice but to publish, as it was burning a hole in my brain, hopefully now I can turn off the constant noise. Until the second book gets its claws into me at least.

Sculpting Amanda

Chapter 1

A.

So, off I go, pad in hand, to start the first day of my new glittering career. Ahead of me, I envisioned office soiree and extended business trips, to Paris or Madrid. My new boss will obviously be tall, dark and brooding, with an undercurrent of dangerous.

At first, I expect he will bark commands and dictations, not taking the time to acknowledge the English rose quality of my beauty, and the innocent naivety that comes with being seventeen, and fresh out of typing college.

Who am I kidding. The only reality of that previous statement is, I am in fact seventeen. "English rose beauty" equates to English and pimpled, almost as though I have had a fight with a rose bush, but that's as close as I came.

I am however starting a new job today. I'm not quite fresh out of typing college because that would suggest it was the nineteen fifties. So, seventeen and fresh from the job centre on North Street. "pad in hand" is a rough map directing me, past the bus garage, left onto Tanner Road and, if my sources are correct, the second building on the right, and up the metal staircase, I should find a blue door. Behind the blue door should be my brooding new boss. According to Tam at the job Centre, his name is Mr Mason, his main requirement for this position was must be able to type sixty words a minute and have a good telephone manner. I'm not overly sure of my typing speed but I can operate a telephone and I am sure I can do it in a good manner.

Perhaps now would be a good time to give you some background story.

I have established I am seventeen and on a job search, I was hoping to get away for a bit longer without getting a real job, but since my sister's bloke got banged up there are fewer babysitting gigs, my sister prefers to wallow in self-pity at the injustice that her beloved "Dale" would be detained at her majesty's pleasure, for something as minor as a parking fine.

I wouldn't go as far as to say he was a hardened criminal, petty at best, however, he had been silly enough to get on the local police radar. It was inevitable that he would get caught eventually. We were all equally surprised something as minor as an unpaid parking fine would escalate to three months inside. My sister chose to ignore the original parking fine as it was outside Chanelle's house and Dale refused to pay it, as to pay it would be to acknowledge he was parked at Chanelle's house.

As you can see it's a dilemma for both parties, as Chanelle is known around these parts as a bit of a good time girl and a man stealer.

So, as I was saying no babysitting gigs equates to no money, mobile phones had been around a while and now they were becoming more accessible.

Two of my friends had recently got one each, they spent hours boasting about what level they were on, on Snakes. They would call me at home from the shop, on the way over to ask if I wanted anything.

To me, it was the opening to a whole new level of independence. I desperately wanted to be part of their gang. No money means, off I trot pad in hand looking for the blue door which could well be my destiny to my very own mobile device.

Mr Mason was a short man; I am five foot and he was a few inches taller. So much for tall, dark and brooding. He was dark, with a shock of white hair. Almost as though he had been involved in an unfortunate incident in a gloss factory and he just couldn't wash it out. I would age him at about forty, but my ageing radar was not very finely tuned, I could just about tell if people were older or younger than me.

He had an incredibly deep voice for such a small man. Squashing any ill-informed assumption that deep voices belong to tall, overpowering men. He was very well spoken and quite eloquent, to coin a phrase "he was not from around these parts" Other than his hair and voice there was little else of interest about him. I was shown to a table that had a computer and two telephones. One blue and one black. I also had a headset so I could type and take calls at the same time.

I had to hold in the excitement as I knew full well these headphones would transport me into Madonna mode. She was in the middle of her Vogue tour and whilst the pointy boobs were not quite mainstream with this headset I could give her a run for her money.

Mr Mason presented me with a text which he asked that I copy, so he could assess my typing speed. I tried to put on a brave face but he knew under his scrutiny I would under perform.

It looked like I would be waving that Nokia goodbye. Several failed attempts to turn the PC on meant I was not off to a good start. Forty-two words per minute with only a sixty-seven percent accuracy score meant I was anything but confident this job would be mine. Fortunately, Mr Mason was lenient. He said he knew from my previous telephone call to him from the job Centre that my telephone manner was satisfactory.

His suggestion was that I practice. By way of practice, he suggested I write a short diary every morning explaining my day.

So here it is, day one my first attempt at a diary to increase my typing speed. File save, save as Mandy private, Mr Mason told me this would mean it was now for me and my eyes only.

Chapter 2

File open, Mandy private, open

M.

I knew she was young and naive but I literally couldn't believe my luck when she agreed to keep a diary on the work PC. Seventeen and other than school, she had no access to a computer, naive enough to think that her words would be private.

Her description of me was minimal but I liked that I factored into her day.

I also gathered from her diary that she didn't remember me. I have met her before, of course, I have, about two years previously. I first set eyes on her whilst I was having a "business meeting" with a shady character from Queens Road, Dale was his name, she was minding his kids at the time.

I was almost struck dumb when I saw her. It was a struggle to carry on the conversation I was having, I was so distracted. It was as though time stood still, nothing mattered in the world at that moment in time but her. It had been an overcast day but the sun seemed to come out just to shine upon her. Illuminating her specifically for my attention.

I would age her at around fourteen or fifteen but she looked young for her age. Her clothes seemed baggy not yet being aware of her assets, at ease in her skin, a tiny slip of a girl her dirty blonde hair braided in plaits. Her plaid maroon skirt and navy blazer giving away details of her secondary school. A brief encounter barely registering on her radar, a man on the outskirts of her vision.

The next time I saw her was a fluke, I'm sure I sensed her first.

I was in my local shopping Centre being dragged around on a mundane shopping trip for shoes or a bag or whatever other status purchase my wife insisted she needed to ensure she was a real player, a force to be reckoned with.

She believed that the newest designer handbag would secure her a place in the elite "wife's club". I humoured her of course, I always did, when in reality I struggled to hide the way I found her vulgar, her appearance repulses me, her arms flapped when she moved her arse was so full and round, she tried to appear educated but often appeared foolish. All of which I pretended not to notice. It was in the shoe department whilst she was squeezing her trotter into yet another red pair of heels that the hairs on my arms stood up on end.

My heart missed a beat I know this as I questioned my own wellbeing. It was then I saw her, she was with a few other girls of her age, chatting and giggling, as young girls often do. I don't know why but I instinctively stepped back into the shadows so she couldn't see me. Hoping I would blend away out of her vision.

I wanted to watch her uninterrupted without fear of being caught.

"darrrrling what do you think of these?"

The spell was broken as the troll demanded more of my attention. I was met with a hideous pair of feet squeezed into a pair of black stilettos, causing her to tower over me bringing her over inflated breast to my eye level,

"Stunning, sweetheart you should buy them" my well rehearse response.

I saw her leaving tiny hips swaying as she walked away. Against my better judgement, I needed to know where she was going. I made my excuses and followed at a distance.

She and her friends went into a burger bar to indulge in greasy fattening food. I was close enough to the car park, on a whim, I went to my car took a fuse out, this meant one of the lights flashed on the dash.

I had every intention now things were in motion to use the car fault as an excuse to pull over or maybe lose the troll whilst I went for a mundane repair.

To my amusement things went to plan the leaving of the shopping Centre was timed well enough that I could spot the girls at the bus stop. Tiny carrier bags filled with whatever treats their measly pocket money allowed them to buy.

The key was put into the ignition and to my surprise, a fault light appeared on the dash. Time for my rehearsed speech "sweetheart the car has a problem, take my card get another bag to match your new shoes and I will find a local garage and be back in an hour"

There was no argument any excuse to have free rain with the gold card the greedy bitch that she was.

The bus was followed but it was painstakingly slow. She finally disembarked forty minutes later. It was a rundown area that I knew vaguely. The bus stop was situated alongside a row of shops consisting of an off license, betting shop and a pizza parlour. Again, a slow laborious stake out took place finishing at a small terraced house with mismatched net curtains and a front door that was well overdue painted.

I took note of the door number and road name, replaced the fuse and drove back to the shopping Centre. My pulse was racing and I was buzzing with the new knowledge I had required.

A.

Day two in my new position and I'm sitting at my desk trying to recall the pin details to retrieve any overnight message that may have been left on the phone. Mr Mason appeared in the doorway and suggests I have an hour typing practice as he has some dictation for me today.

So here I am practice, practice, practice. From what I can make out this is a concession to a larger import and export company that operates from Bristol. Yesterday consisted of a few laborious letters to suppliers, all figures and quantities details for unknown purchases, all of which I knew nothing about.

There were a few phone calls that I answered on Mr Mason's behalf playing the part of his secretary. Mr Mason spent most of his time in his office with his head down. On the few occasions, he did leave the office I noticed he was wearing a very distinctive aftershave. The smell stirred a memory or reaction as sometimes only smells can but for the life of me, I couldn't place where I knew the smell from.

At around three, Mr Mason left the office and returned half an hour later with a coffee and a muffin for me, perks of the job apparently. I could get used to this. I left at four thirty and went home before settling down on the sofa to watch neighbours and home and away.

Eight thirty start today had me rushing for the bus it wouldn't do to be late on my second day, I already have plans for my first week's wages. It doesn't pay too badly as I have no real outlay two hundred quid a week.

I must give mum some money, of course, she is struggling a lot since she chucked dad out but I would like to get the mobile phone I had promised myself first. Mum has already said the first month's wages are mine to do with as I please.

I'm definitely going to need some more office friendly outfits. My interview suit had an airing yesterday and by my reckoning, all I have left are a few school shirts and a pair of black trousers left to wear.

Right, enough of my ranting I have real work to do

File, save, Mandy private

M.

I couldn't wait until she arrived this morning, after having her so close in the office yesterday the sixteen hours we were apart seemed too long.

I collected my usual outfit from the lock up. I got the idea eighteen months back when I first followed her home. The pizza shop close by lent itself perfectly to a disguise. A pizza delivery driver wouldn't get a second glance and the motorcycle helmet helped to cover my mallard's streak.

I waited up the street from her house and see her leave flustered and panicked her face an enduring shade of pink. Her running for the bus in an effort not to be late for her second day alerted me to just how clueless she was.

Racing to the office to be there before she arrived I composed myself, taking a deep breath I allowed my heart rate to slow to a normal pace. Today I would be playing boss man again, a tiny thrill ran through me as I see her approach on the CCTV at the bottom of the staircase.

The offices we were in were described as small but functional by the letting agents. My description was mouldy and cold. I was limited with what was available I needed something that she could access by public transport if I was going to get her here at all.

So far things were going to plan seeing her flushed and running this morning confirmed she needed this job and ensured that I would get to spend more time with her. A bonus to the office being so run down and dilapidated meant that I could justify securing CCTV in most of the rooms. Most of my day yesterday was spent watching her on my PC whilst she typed away. Her beautiful formed hands attempting to keep up with the speed of my dictation; a fruitless task as I was purposely speaking faster than needed. Hoping to get her flustered. The flush of red across her chest as she struggled to complete the impossible.

"Good morning Amanda, I'm glad you're on time"

I couldn't help the little snipe and had to hold in the grin that was threatening to split my face. The diary was something I was looking forward to today and I wasted no time suggesting she "practised" her typing.

The anticipation of the outcome was almost too much my jittered nerves almost giving away my excitement. I decided to leave the office in search of some good coffee.

Two steaming coffees in hand I took the opportunity to slip a laxative into Amanda's cup before entering back into the building. It was a simple enough task removing the plastic coating I emptied the powder in and gave it a stir for good measure.

She had put a bit of weight on over the last eighteen months, not much but enough to take on more of a womanly figure. The bonus of having her so close meant I could help her lose those curves.

I was pleased to see her diary input was saved and decided to spend the morning reading through her take on yesterday. I was slightly alarmed that she thought enough of my aftershave to write about it. I knew instinctively when she had been close enough to me, to remember me, how could I forget!

Two weeks after, I had followed her home and got her address and I decided my interest in this girl had to be explored further. The moped was bought with the authentic pizza box attached, at first, I watched her in the afternoon as she ambled down her street on her way back from school. Watching as she smiled and chatted with her friends. They separated at the bridge and the last ten minutes she walked alone.

Sometimes she listened to her Walkman on her head nodding to an unknown beat. A few days of this led to me waiting by the school in the morning to see her arriving. In the back of my mind, I knew what I was doing would be considered wrong but to be frank I didn't care. I was a thirty-seven-year-old self-made man. I had more money than I could possibly spend. I mixed in enough circles to know that I could do pretty much what I wanted and when I wanted.

There were of course lines that weren't to be crossed regardless of bank balance. There were people out there that considered themselves humane and law abiding. It was these people that would frown upon my interest in this girl, consider it wrong. I had the sense to be discreet and I had no intention of shouting my intentions from the roof top. However, I had intentions bad intentions and I couldn't wait to start the process of becoming part of this girl's life.

Three months I waited, sometimes watching from her school locked away in a workmen's van, not much call for a pizza at 8 am. During the afternoons, I waited for her to arrive home, I started to learn her routine Friday nights; she would meet up with her friends and drink cheap cider.

There were boys in her circle too I had to sit and watch as she threw her head back and laughed at their jokes, flirting her way into their affections. I saw her childish attempts at being sexy or appealing.

I often had to fight back the urge to pull boys off her on nights when she was drunk and pinned to a wall by a barely pubescent spotty teen. I sat in the shadows knuckles white as I battled not to run and pull them off her as they kissed and groped in darkened corners.

There were nights when her mother was out that a boy would go home with her. On these nights, I would have no choice but to go home and bury myself in my whore of a wife to try to forget about her.

These nights were made worse by my pathetic wife mistaking my arousal as being a result of her actions. Her animalistic moans making me sick to the stomach as I pumped away at her disgusting curvaceous body. It was after such a night I decided enough was enough; I couldn't continue with this charade anymore, I needed to have this girl. The obsession was too much I needed to have her and get her out of my system.

My homework done, I knew that Amanda's mother was going to be away for the night. This meant Dean or Dan or whatever his name is would be at her house. I waited in the off-license cap drawn down.

I had made the switch with the vodka before she arrived I knew what brand she would buy. She passed me on the way to the booze section, close enough that I could smell her perfume. Some kind of peach concoction, I remember it being fitting the smell evoking the Promise of youthful fresh flesh.

I moved to stand behind a shelf; I saw her make her purchase and scurry out still a little conscious. She would get stopped and ID at any minute.

I watched her leave the shop, biding my time knowing she was going home. Purchasing a newspaper to avoid any suspicion I strolled back to the parked van. Taking one last look at her house before I climbed into the back. Putting on my earphones I relaxed as best I could.

The timing needed to be just right. I couldn't leave it to chance the week before the "local council" had been to check the fire alarms and the house was bugged. It was costly but I used a discreet company telling them it was my house and I suspected my wife was having an affair. I listened to the chatter in the house and my excitement grew.

Looking around the darkened quiet street I was pleased to see it was empty. The only signs of life were the television lights illuminating from the living room windows. My heart rate quickened as I anticipated the silence which would let me know my opportunity had come. I heard as they giggled and fumbled. Again, fighting the urge to get him away from my girl but knowing that there would be less questions asked if she thought she had been fucking her boyfriend.

Finally, silence fell onto the house the Rohypnol doing its job. Climbing from my hiding place I made my way towards the back gate. Checking around me one last time before I threw my bag over. Once the bag was over it was my turn to scale the gate, quickly and silently I climbed over landing at the bottom with a fud. Eager to get to my prize I scurried toward the back door.

Fortunately, the back door to her house was open. I had a glass cutter in my bag but was glad I never needed to use it. It was a much smoother operation if no questions were asked after. The kitchen was small and grimy, unwashed pans adorned the work surface. The remains of what appeared to be shepherd's pie sat on a baking tray.

The Listening devices I had used to monitor Amanda's activity had been left in the van, I could only hope they were still unconscious when I got to her room. Taking the stair two at a time I reached the top quickly. Calming myself I reached for the door handle. Pushing it open I flinched as the hinges squeaked in protest.

I found them both in her bedroom. Typical of a teenager's room, posters on the wall of her current crush. A dressing table with homework shrewd across it. Moving toward the two still, forms they appeared to be asleep clothing haphazardly covering their bodies. Dressed in a hurry as they both realised they were "much drunker" than usual. Unceremoniously I pulled Dan/Dean away from the bed.

He was heavier than he looked, exerting myself I dragged him onto the landing closing the door. Moving back toward the bed I took in the sight before me. My own heartbeat was thundering in my ears. Standing over Amanda's tiny frame I was suddenly truly grateful that I had the time, money and devotion to partake in this pleasure. Leaning over her I inhaled. Seeking her perfume, it was marred now. Not as fresh as before.

I pulled her down the bed so she was completely flat on her back. She was so light so slight and deliciously delicate. A used condom on the side, told me she had been sexual with the kid. My thundering heartbeat made it difficult for me to hear.

Tilting my head to the side I listen for any movement from the other side of the door. Peeling away her clothes the excitement built inside me. I needed to be closer to her, I lowered myself onto her taking in the scent of her hair, inhaling the breath she exhaled. So, small but so warm I ached for her now.

The blood rushed from my ears is no longer a deafening sound, instead, a pulsing need between my legs that needed to be released. My face buried in her neck; she tasted salty with a hint of the vodka that had helped to render her so helpless.

Once more checking over my shoulder to ensure the coast was clear I took my opportunity. I undone my fly and rested my aching cock at her opening but it was too much just touching her flesh with mine broke me, an instant spasm ripped through me, my hot seed spilling over her before I had a chance to enter her. This wasn't how I had planned it, my intention was to have her but the sheer closeness and promise of her was enough to have me undone. Just like the teenage lover I had thrown to one side I had reverted to a young boy again. Embarrassed by my behaviour. Even without a witness to judge me I felt ashamed at how easily I had reached my peak. I needed to clean her up. Fortunately, I had come prepared. I never intended to leave a trace. I wiped away the evidence. Delicate and gentle afraid that I might damage her somehow, being this close to her Centre caused me to stiffen again. This time I was going to penetrate her, I needed to stop this now; I was aware it was too much it was all consuming.

I took her that night not once but twice as her tiny, frail body swayed to my punishing beat. When I was satisfied, I dressed her. Tidying up her hair and positioning her onto the bed as though she was a princess sentenced to sleep by a wicked witch. For a moment, I reflected upon the irony. The reality was she had been sentenced to sleep, not by a wicked witch, but by me a man with wicked intentions. Going back to the door I put my ear to it listening for any movement from the boy. Met with more silence, I pulled him back into the room by his feet. His tee shirt bunching at his back as I pulled him, dumping him next to her bed, I gave him a swift kick for good measure. He groaned in response but remained unconscious. Leaving the room, I retreated as quickly as I could.

So, there it is the full sordid story of why she knew my aftershave, she might not recall, but I had been all over her body taking my fill of her and enjoying her flesh with my body and tongue. She would wake a little more tender perhaps even sore, but she would assume Dean had been a little more adventurous than usual, almost two years on the memory of that night had been replayed in my mind again and again.

 Assuming it had been a faultless operation, it was only now reading her diary entry I realised I hadn't factored my own scent into things I thought I had been so clever, so thorough at covering my tracks.

A.

 Day three, yesterday was a strange day my guts were all over the place, desperate to not make it too obvious my innards were falling out; I tried to make my visits to the toilet discreet. Fortunately, the loos were up on the top floor of the building. It must have been something I had eaten. As a result, I skipped lunch, no fuel no waste, right?

Deli belly aside Mr Mason left the office shortly after three and didn't come back until just before I left at four thirty. My knowledge of him is minimal, but he seemed a little angry; he carried himself differently his face was dark with unexploded rage. I hope he wasn't angry with me due to my many toilet brakes.

Today I decided against breakfast I don't want the deli belly making a reappearance. I ate very little, to be honest just stuck to water from the office kitchen and the coffee Mr Mason brought me back. My plans were foiled though as my stomach remained very unsettled. If this keeps up, I would have to visit the quacks.

Day 4

It was a busy day yesterday my diary entry was short mostly due to lots of Madonnaesk headset action, due to the continuous phone calls I received. I still love the headset I don't think I will ever tire from the vogue moves I get to pull when Mr Mason isn't looking. I was early this morning partly because I chose to miss breakfast again.

The door was locked as Mr Mason was yet to arrive. The weather was awful, so I took shelter under the metal staircase. Five minutes of avoiding a local tsunami then Mr Mason pulled up. Walking around to the front of the steps he signalled for me to walk up ahead of him, as I passed him onto the metal staircase he rested his hand on the small of my back. It was nothing sleazy just a gentle assistance as I passed him.

I know it's cliché, but my stomach did a little flip. Granted he is older than me by a billion years, but he does have a kind face and the most beautiful eyes. Ooh eeer get your womb in check Mandy, I'm not even sure if he is married I assume he is he wears a ring.

Special request from Mr Mason to practice, practice, practice my typing speed with diary entries. I thought my typing speed had made progress but apparently not. Right, what can I write about now? Not much to report my sister was at ours last night with the kids moping and groaning. Dale's lawyer had been in contact whilst he had been inside the police had uncovered some evidence regarding a local business that was held at gun point; Dale's fingerprints were found, and he was being fingered for armed robbery. Looked like another six years could be added to his sentence.

I felt sad for her of course I do but she made her bed with that man, he has never been anything other than trouble. It was that which attracted her to him to start with, two kids, later and looking at six years of waiting for him as the dutiful wife the lifestyle suddenly doesn't seem so appealing. My sister's life is enough to put me off boys for a while.

I don't want that for myself pregnant at eighteen and tied down to a local playboy. Not that I can have kids, a misjudged night with my ex Dean saw to that. Fifteen and incredibly drunk we were caught semi-naked and unconscious by my mum. Way too much vodka had led to a blackout something I'm prone to because of being five foot nothing and seven stone

We must have canned it that night though as Dean was out for the count as well. Six weeks after waking up with my mum standing over us I was rushed to the hospital, GOD the pains were unbearable; stomach cramps and leg pains with each cramp I had a shooting pain up into my shoulders. I had spent the morning feeling very unwell.

I couldn't find comfort, no matter what I tried. It was during a history lesson I stood to go to the toilet, and my vision dimmed. My heartbeat was racing frantically in my ears. My clothes seemed to instantly soak with sweat, the last thing I remembered was a ringing in my ears and a blackness. I had fainted at school and was admitted to the local hospital in an ambulance. Ectopic pregnancy was the diagnoses. If I had arrived at the hospital half an hour later, I would have bled out.

Internal bleeding was caused by my fallopian tube to tear. This had to be removed rendering me infertile. Dean had been out of the picture since my mum had caught us, his parents had moved him to a different school. I was fifteen, he was seventeen they were worried my mum would get him arrested. She wasn't above threatening it as she marched him home on the day in question.

She may have been a small woman, but she had no qualms dragging his sorry ass back home that morning. As he had moved away, I never did get the chance to ask him how it happened if I recall correctly we always used protection. Sad story but if nothing else by putting it on paper I improve my typing skills it's a win, right?

File, save Mandy private

M.

I'm enjoying having Amanda as my captive, she may not realise it but as each day goes by I'm closer to my ultimate goal, controlling her. I've continued to put the laxative into her coffees and am anticipating the delicious results the lack of nourishments will cause her body.

I feel a need to up the ante a little with each passing day I need to own her again. Initially, my intention was to have her and get her out of my system. This was flawed, instead of getting my fill and reverting to my previous life of getting my kicks by paying a few selected whores; I found it only increased my appetite for her more.

Initially, I spent a few weeks battling myself and my urges to just grab her off the street and take her away with me, lock her up and keep her for myself. My disguises were being overused; I was in danger of revealing myself. I had so many scenarios going through my head; none of them beneficial to anyone but me.

There was one sticking point if I abducted her then she would be missed, I couldn't risk being found; I needed a fool proof plan.

Round and round I went in my own head driving myself mad. Eventually, I had no choice but to activate a self-imposed absence. My businesses were micro-managed by selective trusted employees, but they needed my attention. I had been obsessed with her for far too long, and it was becoming detrimental to my companies, my mind, and freedom. I was on the verge of doing something silly and breaking cover I knew I couldn't afford to be careless.

I needed six months, six months away from her to rid myself of the obsession if after six months she was still so entwined in my mind I would have to activate plan B.

I went away, myself and the troll, we travelled to city after city securing business deals and fraternising with high society. To my amusement, the troll come into her own at these events many a man's eyes were seen to follow her when she entered a room, I put myself in their shoes tried to see what they saw. Five foot eleven, hour glass figure, a tiny waist with ample bosoms and a round arse. All hair, tits and teeth.

I saw how the men coveted her and looked at me with envy when she was on my arm. She was all women and knew it. I can't deny heads turn when my wife enters a room she ticks all the boxes, such a shame the boxes were not mine.

On the nights when she was receiving the most attention, I managed to use the envy as an aphrodisiac. It was these nights I took pleasure in groping at her soft round behind and claiming her in front of all the other testosterone driven men. Occasionally kissing her on the mouth when she lent in for affection. Nights like this that my body would react slightly to what everyone else found attractive in her.

It always started well a flicker of arousal giving me the confidence to reach out to her and signal my intentions, but as soon as she replicated and began to sigh her breath catching in her throat, her chests heaving as her excitement became apparent. Off come her clothes revealing what some men would describe as perfect all starlet and Jessica rabbit curves; it was then I would begin to lose interest. I couldn't disguise my disgust some nights, her giant tits and curvy hips the vile way she waxed and styled her dark pubic hair into ridiculous landing strips. Her ruby red talon nails which she would run across my back.

All of this disgusted me no matter how much male envy-driven testosterone had surrounded us during the evening. I could no longer rely upon that to get me through the ordeal. Instead, I thought of Amanda so small, so frail lying still and accommodating. This was the only way I could perform for my wife; the only way I could block out the feel of her soft fleshy body beneath mine.

I had to pretend the curvy hips were Amanda's bony one's, kid myself that her body was, in fact, childlike and perfect instead of over pumped and fleshy. Sometimes it worked, but other times it didn't, on these occasions I may have broken my facade long enough to tell her she was too fat, too loud, too tall. I never waited for her reaction just threw a wad of cash in her direction and left, off to find a prostitute that was young enough or thin enough to fool my disappointed cock into a climax.

I stayed away for seven months in total; I needed to be sure that I had given myself the chance to get her out of my system. If plan B had to be put into place, I needed to know I had tried every other option first. Plan B was no walk in the park it would be a massive lifestyle change.

I had had seven months to come up with it. Delusional that I would forget her in that time I had instead spent most of my time fantasising about ways to have her again.

It needed to be as fool proof as possible. First things first, I needed to get her brother-in-law out of the way. I could no longer spend my time with her hidden behind disguises and shadows. It was time to make my entrance.

Dale was an easy pawn to remove a few calls to the right people, and he was out of the way for a while. I couldn't risk him blowing my cover should he ever realise the boss of her small import company was, in fact, the same person he reported to regularly regarding a sideline of money laundering, I'm sure a few questions would have been asked.

Next, the building was secured, and plans were put in place for her to be lined up for an interview. Tamwah at the local job Centre and myself had a mutual interest. His desire to be watched and my willingness to be part of that voyeurism meant our paths had crossed several times at a whore house or two across the country.

A few persuasive words in his ear convinced him his wife didn't need to know about his extramarital affairs. With Tamwah on board no one else but him, myself and Amanda knew about the convenient local opening for a typist.

So here I find myself almost two years in the making, she's a little older a tad less innocent but still as vulnerable and frail as I remember her. The real icing on the cake I only had to touch her, and the silly little thing is developing feelings for me. Now's the time for the real games to begin.

Chapter 3

A.

Day 5, end of the working week that wasn't too bad I suppose I can think of worse ways to make money. My stomach bug doesn't seem to be settling anytime soon I missed breakfast again today, I did have dinner last night but couldn't eat too much; I think my stomach is shrinking due to the lack of food.

I have already lost weight in my boobs which is typical I barely have an A cup. Hopefully, I will feel up to eating tonight. I have plans to go out with a few of the girls to town, I need to eat before I go don't want to be drinking on an empty stomach. I'm not sure what to wear I got a cute dress from Tammy girl. I can rarely buy clothes in the adult section as I'm pretty small which is fine but there aren't many cute and sexy outfits in the kid's department, so I tend to fall back on jeans and a tee. Oooh hang on movement from the bosses' office, be right back.

"Amanda, can you call this number for me and reserve two tickets to a conference they have next weekend ",

"Yes Mr Mason",

"It's an overnight conference in Edinburgh do you think you can attend as my plus one? I will need you to take notes for me throughout the day, there is an evening meal, but Sunday is yours to do with as you please till we have to fly back. Is it something you think you could attend?"

"erm ... yes sure I don't have any plans ",

"Excellent, oh Amanda I almost forgot in the top drawer of your desk is a mobile phone, it's technically billed to the office but I don't see why you can't use it for personal use, it's not to be used during office time of course"

Day 5, part 2

Fudging hell Mr Mason wants me to go to a soiree with him! Opening my top drawer and what do I see a brand new mobile phone! Sodding hell I could make a mills and boon story out of this job yet! Watch this space.

I went straight home from work and sat down to transfer the numbers from my phone book into the mobile. The office number was already saved alongside a few suppliers that's we often liaise with. I also noticed Mathew Mason in the contacts.

As ridiculous as it sounds Knowing his Christian name made him seem more approachable. I navigated my way around the mobile with ease and took great pleasure in texting my friends notifying them of my new mobile number.

I also took the time to search through the newspaper for the ringtone codes. I decided on "flava" by Peter Andre.

With the radio blaring, I decided to get ready for my night out, a warm bath and hair wash later I decided on a piece of dry toast for tea. Another day of rushing to the loo meant I couldn't face a big dinner. Makeup done and slipping into some ballet pumps I was ready for the off, texting Bella as I made my way to the bus stop to let her know I was on my way to hers.

Bella greeted me at the door with alcoholic concoction which instantly went to my head. My limbs felt a little looser my head a little lighter, I loved how booze made me feel, it always made me feel a little more confident, made me feel a little taller, more attractive. I should learn my limits though there had been a few too many nights my memory was vague, and others where I couldn't remember a thing. My friends were full of stories of how I danced on tables and tried to snog random boys.

I should try to get a handle on it, maybe I would start next time as tonight already looked like it was going to be a heavy one.

We got into the club, as usual, Bella and Nell got in no questions, I got ask for ID yet again the curse of always looking twelve., Dale wasn't good for many things, but I was grateful when he managed to set me up with a fake ID.

The place was heaving jamiroquai pumping out of the speakers, we had to squeeze our way pass the dance podiums where girls gyrated in knee high fur boots and bikinis. Glow sticks aloft swaying to the music.

I see a few of Dales friends moving amongst the crowd no doubt supplying the E and speed to get the party started. The bar was three deep as we made our way over to try to buy some shots. Mark Morrison rang out loud, and I stood back and surveyed my surroundings. From where I was standing I could just make out the VIP lounge.

I was shocked when I saw Mr Mason seated at a table sipping cocktails. My stomach flipped with excitement, he was out of his suit and in a more relaxed outfit of open shirt and jeans he looked much younger. He was chatting with some men and to his left with her arm draped a crossed his shoulder was the most beautiful amazon of women. She was stunning, watching her move to the music was mesmerising. She was so graceful. The pair of them together were breathtaking. I couldn't help but feel my stomach drop.

This must be his wife. This was confirmed as he casually slipped his hand up onto her exposed knee. I felt so foolish watching them, so angry for allowing myself to develop a crush on him. There was no way I could compete with such a beautiful woman. I was glad I had seen them together before I had been silly enough to act upon my new-found affection for him.

M

I was watching when Amanda entered the club. I had been eagerly awaiting her arrival for the last hour. Not much was by chance anymore I knew she would come here, she often did. It had not been easy to engineer this particular train of events.

Getting the troll to agree to attend such a down and out place had been a struggle. It wasn't often she liked to be seen on the east side of town, it wasn't glitzy or glamourous enough. I fabricated some story about having to meet some important business investors here; her attendance was cemented with the promise we wouldn't stay long. We were booked into an elusive hotel for the evening as a treat for her compliance.

Once I saw Amanda make her way to the bar I learnt into my wife encouraging her to become more affectionate.

By the time Amanda spotted us, my wife was making a fool of herself by lounging all over me. It took a lot of good acting on my part to reach out and caress my wife's leg. All for Amanda's benefit, I needed her to see just how very insignificant she was to a "big fish" like me.

I wondered if Amanda would make herself known to me but she didn't she threw herself into the drink, shot after shot. I watched from afar for half an hour then came good on my promise to my wife. We left and caught a taxi.

I couldn't help but realise the irony. I was walking out of the club to spend the night with someone whom most would consider a beautiful woman when the only person I wanted to spend the night with was tucked up in a corner half drunk and drowning in crippling doubt and self-pity.

A.

I watched Mr, and Mrs Mason leaves, she was stunning. It was as though her beauty made him more appealing. As a couple, they were gorgeous.

He was a little shorter than most Hollywood stars, but they had that air about them. They were like Richard Gere and Cindy Crawford. Her dress with like a second skin emphasising every curve. Cut low to expose her pert large boobs. In short, she was everything I wasn't. I stared at the back of his head willing him to turn and look at me, I don't know why? Maybe just for acknowledgement.

I wanted him to turn and smile, or wave, anything? I knew I was being a fool, but I realised I was suddenly desperate for the smallest scrap of attention from him. Once he left, I canned the ouzo, I have a vague memory of dancing with a friend of Dales. James, I think his name was, I remember him placing a pill on my tongue.

I danced till closing time. He was rubbing himself against me as the music slowed. I remember going back to his place but after that nothing?

The sun shining through my enclosed curtains woke me. Fortunately, I was at home, I seemed to have acquired a grazed elbow, my head was banging.

I have had enough blackouts to know what checks to make in an effort to piece a night together, the first check would be to work out if I have had sex. In this instance, it seemed I hadn't. Which was a bonus. I heard a strange beep, it took me a while to register it was my phone. It was a text from Bella. Apparently, I had made a fool of myself at James's house, tearful and incoherent, he had driven me home, disappointed that his sure thing was too drunk to walk let alone fuck.

Peanut butter on toast was all I could face to squash the thunderous hangover. Fortunately, it stayed down. It managed to stay in as well which is a real bonus of late, perhaps I was finally coming to the end of this stomach bug.

Whilst checking out my reflection in the bathroom mirror, I decided to get mums scales and check my weight. My face looked gaunt, and my eyes had dark circles under them, mostly due to my hangover, but I was sure I had also lost weight. My fears were confirmed when I stepped on the scales six stone eleven pounds. Thanks to a dodgy belly I had lost five pounds in less than a week. I couldn't afford to lose one let alone five.

Going to the kitchen, I decided to stockpile some crisps and chocolate for the rest of the day.

The day was wasted in the end. I spent it in the fetal position praying the peanut butter on toast wouldn't make a reappearance.

My body had fooled me initially into thinking I never had a hangover. I fed my face quite happily believing I was lucky enough to have consumed so much ouzo and come away unscathed, it was half an hour later that the hangover decided to appear. It started with the pounding headache being exchanged for a full-scale drum solo by Phil Collins, this would have been fine, but Phil had decided to rent my skull as his recordings space.

Whilst my head pounded to catastrophic proportions, my stomach lurched along to the beat. God, I feel ill! Will I ever learn!

By the evening the prospect of a night in front of casualty and London's burning was enough to give me the incentive to leave the house. I made my way to Nell's hangover still fresh in my mind I decided that I wasn't going to drink.

Nell's parents were away, but her older brother was home, at twenty Nell's parents considered him responsible enough to play house whilst they were away. They couldn't have been more wrong. Liam was at best a complete stoner, at worst a coked-up stone roses wanna be. Tonight, he had friends over, I could hear the music from the bus stop, oasis singing away.

Nell came to the door and tried her best to signal a warning before I got into the living room.

My addled brain had difficulty processing what she was trying to relay. It wasn't until I got through the door I realised she was warning me that James from the night club was present. "Oh bollocks"

It slipped out before I had a chance to realise I was going to say it.

"Charming, nice to see you too babe," was James response.

"Sorry, it wasn't directed at you, I just remembered ... I've left my key in doors."

I think he bought it as no more was said about my unconventional greeting.

Fortunately, James was a quite good company, I learnt that he only "worked" the clubs at weekends, A bit of extra cash to supplement his student lifestyle, He was studying economics and accounting. We chatted most of the night, I kept the promise to myself that I wouldn't drink, but I did partake in a few Es courtesy of James stash.

The conversation flowing and not wanting the night to end I called mum and told her I was going to spend the night at Nell's. This translated as I was gonna bunk up with James on the sofa.

I woke up Sunday with a clear head. I didn't need to do the usual check after a night with a boy to work out if I had slept with him, I knew I had, in fact, he was still snoring away beside me. I crawled over him and an effort to get off the sofa before I woke him.

I hadn't been drinking last night, but I still had the breath of a thousand camels. I needed to brush my teeth and fast. Once I come back downstairs from freshening up James was starting to stir seeing me at the door he turned smiled and pulled me in for a quick fumble before the rest of the house woke up. Plans were made to see each other again, and mobile numbers were exchanged.

I skipped home a little brighter that day, seems little ole Mandy may have got herself a boyfriend. Who needed Mr Mason, with his beautiful wife, posh voice and paint stained head?

M.

I managed to get through the weekend relatively unscathed. I had enjoyed my performance at the club but knew that an even greater performance would be expected once my wife and I were locked away in our hotel room.

My wife was flustered and tipsy from the champagne she was pawing at my shirt before we even got into our hotel room. Normally I would push her away and pretend to be tired, but tonight she deserved a treat.

She had behaved well helping me to achieve my directive. When we had left the club, all eyes were on her. From the corner of the bar, Amanda's eyes almost shone green with envy. Pushing her to the bed, I buried my face between her thighs. Fortunately, her sounds of satisfaction were muffled as her thighs gripped at my head, she thrashed her way to an orgasm. Whilst she was building to her climax, I had used my hand to get myself hard enough to penetrate her, all the while thinking of Amanda and the wisps of untamed blonde hair between her legs.

My memory of her was wearing thin I needed her again and soon. For now, I would have to make do. Flipping my wife over me forced my cock into her arse. It was tight and dry, closing my eyes and imagining Amanda as I did.

My wife screamed out as another orgasm ripped through her body. This almost put me off but fortunately, I was close, and I came deep inside her. She slumped satisfied twitching as the remanences of her orgasm petered away. I waited until sleep claimed her; once she was out for the count, I spent half an hour in the shower. Disgusted with the depths I had to sink too.

I let the hot water pound down upon me washing her filth and secretion away.

Sunday went by too slowly I was eager for Monday to come around. Amanda's absence was too raw, just after lunch, I made my excuses and left to return to my old haunt. Two hours I sat positioned across from Amanda's house surveillance equipment activated to hear her shuffling inside the house, from what I could make out she wasn't home some noises and muttering confirmed someone was, I assumed it was her mother.

She finally comes sauntering down the road around two thirty. Her blonde hair hangs loose to her tiny waist, flat pumps denim shorts and a vest top was her outfit of choice. She looked a little whorish for my liking given the choice; I would dress her in something a little less revealing. I found I was gripping my fists so angry that she was dressed the way she was. Flexing my fists to recirculate the blood.

She looked tired, she passed by the van, so close I could almost touch her, it was pleasing for me to see she looked frailer than normal her weight was falling off. She was so close to perfection, she didn't know it, but this weekend she would be mine again this time I would savour my time with her there would be no boyfriend outside the door, no impending return of parents.

It would be just me and her and I was going to take my fill of her whether she liked it or not.

Chapter 4

A.

Monday came with an added bonus of sunshine. It was a blistering hot day from the get go. Unfortunately, my Work clothes were still limited I had a choice of trousers or an old-school skirt. So, I opted for the maroon skirt and matched it with a black vest and my old faithful ballet pumps.

I only hope that Mr Mason wasn't familiar with St Josephine's uniform. Mr Mason was in his office when I arrived he looked up long enough to nod. I could have been imagining it, but he appeared to give me the once over, and a genuine smile split his face.

My ovary actually danced, the effect of that smile had such impact, Fuck I was in trouble, why couldn't it be James that caused such a reaction. Since Friday Mr Mason had morphed into the most desirable man I have ever seen, myself meanwhile must pale into complete insignificant next to his stunning wife.

Sitting at my desk I opened the post for the day, the tickets for the weekend's conference had arrived. We were booked to fly out Friday evening and return late Sunday.

I couldn't help but wonder what his wife would make of his absence, but I imagine she felt little need to be jealous as stunning as she was.

The morning passed by in a blur, I didn't get much chance to write a diary entry the telephone rang relentlessly. Mr Mason left the office and returned with the usual coffee, my stomach rumbled I would have been grateful for the muffin today, but there was none on offer.

I felt compelled to tell Mr Mason I had seen him on Friday evening.

"I saw you Friday evening, in Hollywood's, the nightclub in town."

"Really you should have given me a shout I would have bought you a drink,

Amanda."

"No, it's fine, you didn't stay long, and you were with someone."

"Yes my wife, we had a business meeting, not our usual haunt I must confess, I prefer my carpet less sticky!"

For some reason, I needed to tell him just how beautiful his wife was to ignore it felt deceitful.

"She is very attractive your wife, you are a very lucky man."

"Thank you, Amanda, yes I am."

Handing the post to Mr Mason our hands brushed against each other, from my perspective it actually felt electric, as though a live current ran between us. Mr Mason, however, appeared unaffected.
I really needed to get a rein on my feelings for him they seemed to be developing at an alarming rate. As much as I was a romance novel fan I needed to understand this was real life; if I let my heart rule my head the way it was threatening to then my professionalism would be affected. I knew I was over analysing every look, every word, and every smile.

Mr Mason had given me no reason to believe the feelings were reciprocated, I'm pretty sure if I didn't get a handle on things this job would be short-lived.

M.

It dawned on me early Monday that Amanda needed a lot of work if I was going to display her in public. When I originally booked the conference, it was with myself in mind, an opportunity to get her away for a few nights so I could indulge in my obsession.

The reality was she would be representing myself and the franchises at this conference, we would be mixing with genuine business contacts and potential investors. A seventeen-year-old barely educated undernourished child was not everyone's idea of a poster girl. With only five days to work with, I decided it was time for a bit of "my fair lady" treatment.

I wanted her to be able to hold her own at this conference. She needed to be given the heads up on what to expect and how to behave. Her youth was something I couldn't disguise, however. I just hoped she was a good learner.

Time to put my lustful thoughts aside and do what I do best and talk business.

A.

My plans to squash my growing emotions were completely foiled over the next few days. In an effort to get my knowledge up to scratch for the looming conference Mr Mason spent most days at my desk filling me in on various details that were relevant to the business running and success, he encourages me to take notes and spent hours going over spreadsheets and growth charts. He discussed competitors and investors, shipping agents and brokers. In short, I had the crash course on import and export structures.

By the third day satisfied that my knowledge was coming along well, we broke for lunch. Mr Mason suggested that we ate together at a good restaurant he knew in town. He explained it was quite formal, but it would give me an opportunity to see what would be the accepted behaviour for the forthcoming weekend.

I had visions of the "pretty women" scene where Julia Roberts is eating lobster, and it flies across the table. The reality was a little less daunting. It was a pleasant setting, Mr Mason ordered the wine, and I attempted to decipher the menu which was in French. Mr Mason appeared to be pleasantly surprised when I ordered the food and conversed with the waiter. After ordering our food we sat waiting, I had intentions of sipping the wine it would not do to be inebriated back in the office. Looking up through my lashes again my heart performed a flip he was such an attractive man, I wondered what had changed since I had first met him. I can't believe I thought there was little of interest about him.

I sat watching him covertly, I found myself telling him antidotes and jokes attempting to amuse him. I adored the laughter lines around his eyes and the way he tilted his head slightly to the left as he listened. His hands were large and strong, I suspected his nails were manicured as each nail was perfectly trimmed. Aside from the colour variation, his hair was neatly trimmed, and he was always clean shaven.

Our food was delicious, and the wine flowed. At some point, I became aware that it was getting late.

"Mr Mason should I not be getting back to the office?"

"Amanda its fine I'm the boss remember; you have done so well these last few days you deserve this treat. Enjoy it they don't come often."

I wanted dessert, but Mr Mason suggested we move to the bar instead. My concerns about drinking too much were pushed to one side, and I found myself loosening up. The conversation was flowing.

I was able to determine that Mr Mason was well travelled he had attended University in London. He was well educated and enjoyed playing golf in his spare time. He wanted to know about my family, so I told him and pressed for details about his. "You know a lot about me Mr Mason, how about you, where does your family originate from?" "My mother was from Ireland my father was from Oxford."

"Ireland, well that explains your dark hair, I'm pretty sure I saw a leprechaun in the office yesterday he must have been a relative, where in Ireland is your mother from?"

"Ahh, well that I don't know I'm afraid she died during childbirth, so my knowledge of her is minimal."

"Oh, I'm so sorry Mr Mason, how awful."

"It's fine Amanda these things happen."

"Do they though in this day and age do women still die from childbirth?"

I spoke before I had a chance to think, the wine breaking down the part of my brain that filters out the impolite questions. Fortunately, he took things in is stride making a joke of my loose lips,

"no, your right Amanda it was all a big lie fabricated to make you feel sorry for me, I was hoping for a sympathy fuck."

His words had me choking on my drink and the wink that accompanies it had my heart beat racing,

"My mother was a very small woman, she had a very difficult time birthing my older sister. I was an accident a mistake she was advised not to have any more children, but these things happen. According to an aunt, a caesarian was booked to prevent my mother from going through further trauma, but I came earlier than expected, it was a snowy night, and my father couldn't get her to the hospital in time. I was born, but she died, to be honest, I know little of her my father refused to discuss her with me once I was old enough to ask."

"And your sister Mr Mason do you see much of her?"

It was then I saw genuine sadness in his eyes, just for a passing second it went as quickly as it appeared a smile replacing the hesitation.

"I'm afraid not Amanda, she has also passed away, you're not having much luck with your questions today are you?"

"Oh, my! Again I'm so sorry, do you mind if I ask how?"

There was a pause whilst he decided if he wanted to tell me or not, I could hear a pin drop as I waited for his response.

"She died when I was young about eleven, you remind me of her Amanda! Very much so, you could pass as sisters" my breath caught in my throat as he reached his hand across the bar and stroked my face. Something changed in his stature he softened slightly.

"She was fourteen, her life had been much tormented, she had some mental issues and her and my father's relationship was very tempestuous, she had attempted to take her life on several occasions, both efforts were prevented. In the end, she took things into her own hands, a year before her death she chose to stop eating. Eventually, she just slipped away. Heart failure due to Anorexia was the official cause of death, but it was never a vanity issue. She needed to take back the control refusing to eat meant she got to."

I was so saddened by Mr Masons stories I felt I needed to change the subject. We went on to talk about more trivial things, laughter came easily.

However, in the back of my alcohol fuelled mind, I sensed something of importance had passed between us. Stumbling out of the restaurant I found myself falling into Mr Mason's arms, a typical movie moment. Before I could think I leant in for a kiss. Mr Mason seemed shocked at first and almost kissed me back, but all too quickly he pushed me away.

"Please, Amanda! You have had too much to drink! I'm old enough to be your father not to mention you're still a child why would you think I would be interested."

Even in my drunken state, I found his words cutting, He looked at me like I had shit in his shoe the disdain so evident on his face.

Chapter 5

It's not often I wish for a black out but waking up this morning I so wished I had.

The memory was all too fresh, Mr Mason taking me to a taxi rank and the silence between us as we waited for a taxi to become available. The curt nod of his head as he wished me goodnight and the overwhelming disappointment in myself as I realised just how much I had fucked up.

M.

Thursday morning looms, I have hardly slept a wink. I wonder if Amanda will come into the office today. Nothing like a bit of rejection by the boss to ruin any potential career moves.

It had not crossed my mind pushing her away yesterday how the rejection would pan out. I hadn't factored her leaving into my plans. Sometimes I forget she is a teenager and teenagers are temperamental. It actually took me by surprise when she fell into my arms the way she did, sure I had seen her watching me, and I saw the way she blushed when I caught her.

I knew from her diary entries she had an interest in me but her feeling combined with wine had forced her to show her hand. Her having these feelings for me was something I could only dream of. She was a gift that just kept giving. It took a lot of willpower on my part not to reciprocate her kiss.

I had enjoyed the lunch date she impressed me with her conversation skills. She could hold her own, she was confident and mature in her outlook. She appeared to speak fluent French, from a business point of view that could be very useful. In a different world, we would have been a perfect match. If I was a different man, a better man I may have felt guilty about the future she had in store. Instead, I felt even more excited. She wasn't going to break as easily as I had anticipated.

This turn of events added another aspect to the game, made it more challenging. I relished the challenged she was presenting. I was even more eager to break her. First her body and then her mind.

I got to the office early and sat clock watching, waiting for Amanda to appear. I really hoped I hadn't scared her off I had come this far, so much had been put into place almost every eventuality catered for, I didn't want her pride to be my downfall. Tick tuck went the clock, I heard every stroke.

I sat willing the office door to swing open. She was late it was eight forty, she had never been this late before I could kick myself for not predicting her reaction. Eight forty-five and she falls through the door full of apologies and excuses for her delay. Standing tall, well as tall as a five-foot girl can, she adjusted her clothing smoothed down her wayward hair and proceeded to sit at her desk.

I couldn't help but notice she had paid extra attention to her appearance this morning. Her face was meticulously made up, her blouse was unbuttoned, a tad lower than was acceptable exposing the top of her underwear. A belt nipped in her waist to tiny proportions.

I knew a "fuck you" when I saw one. Here she was dressed to the nines showing me what I had missed out on. She may not have realised that's what she was doing, but ultimately all women work the same. Here she was actively "preening her feathers". Reassured she was in for the long haul I pushed her a little harder.

"Amanda, your typing speed is beginning to let you down. I need you to write a three-hundred-word diary entry. You can choose the subject matter of your choice, but I want it done in under ten minutes. OH, and Amanda button up your shirt your beginning to look desperate",

cutting and derogative was going to be the only game I played this morning, this afternoon I would throw her a few scraps of attention, keep her coming back for more.

A.

For starters three hundred fucking words who does he think he is! (That's twelve, do these counts? these would make it twenty-four) How fucking dare he tell me I looked desperate! So I put a bit of mascara on and took the time to blow dry my hair.

I was late because of it, and the running blew it all into a big tangled mess, but it was for my benefit, not his. Granted I had not taken his rejection well, but I wasn't going to wallow.

A text from James this morning meant I had evening plans hence the extra attention to my appearance. He is blatantly so fucking arrogant he believed it was for his benefit. I have decided to be sensible regarding Mr "fuckwit"

Mason. He is out of my league why I would have believed otherwise is beyond me, I can only assume it was the wine that convinced me that he was bored with the amazon and instead fancied himself a portion of plain Jane.

In all honesty, things are going really well with James. I have met up with him a couple of times since Sunday. We have had a few dates, not just booty calls, He paid for me to go bowling Monday evening, so I think he likes me. I admit he doesn't make my pulse race like the arsehole does, I also find myself pretending it's his lips on mine on a few occasions, but otherwise we are a good match. (Hang on, how many words, two hundred and fifty) Anyway, what was I saying? That's right my boss is an arsehole, and I don't need him in my life other than to pay my wages. I'm going to marry James and live happily ever after, just as long as I refrain from drinking in Mr Mason's presence ever again it should all go perfectly to plan.

Fuck you if it's not enough words I'm stopping as my ten minutes are up!

File, Mandy private save.

M.

File, Mandy private, open

Seriously I leave her alone for five minutes, and the little bitch gets a boyfriend? I shouldn't be, but I'm fuming. I had factored this as a possibility, but I predicted I would see it coming, it's come as a surprise to me. I have no choice now I know she would be susceptible to my affection, I will have to change my plans and reel her in quicker than I would like to. I was so enjoying the whole rejection phase I was hoping to drag it out a little longer.

I put in a call to the florist, my wife would have expected large extravagant, exotic bouquet, but I suspected Amanda had never been bought flowers she seemed like the kind of girl that would be over the moon with a bunch of daisies. I decided to play it safe and order some pink roses and carnations. The message was a little trickier what should it say? Something that conveyed sorrow, I needed to give her hope, make her think there was a chance that something could happen between us. Just enough of a lead that the boyfriend would be put into the back burner.

Amanda, firstly may I apologise for my reactions and punishing words. I am in a very compromising position; I have found myself thinking about you over the past few days. I realise that my intentions were not honourable. I'm more than aware that to become involved with a staff member would be a messy affair. However, I feel I must confess that I found your advances satisfying. If I had not been having my own internal dialogue condemning any relationship potential between us, I fear I would have been weak enough to respond to your attempted kisses. What I am attempting to convey Amanda is that you are a very tempting young lady. I credit my maturity for protecting us both from what could become a very confusing and destructive relationship. As you know, I am married not to mention your employer. Please accept these flowers as an apology but also these words as comfort. You were not misled into believing there was chemistry between us, in a different life we could have pursued it but as things stand it can only be something we dream about. We must be content to admire each other from afar

Mathew

xxx

The burning question was when should I send them? I settled on around four. Just enough time for her to process the meaning before she left the office. If everything went to plan her date tonight would be saturated with thoughts of me.

I left my office, tossing the keys onto Amanda's desk attempting to convey as much nonchalance as possible.

"Lock up please Amanda, come in tomorrow morning I won't be here, man the phones till three. I will send a taxi to bring you to the airport."

"Yes Mr Mason"

Leaving the office, I take a long breath of air filling my lungs with the sweet smell of the lavender that grew quite haphazardly amongst the smog and grit of the city. Today I was going to enjoy the beautiful things life had to offer. I was going to switch off to the film of dirt and sorrow that seemed to be my soundtrack. Tomorrow I would have Amanda, my Amanda, my way and she would cleanse the filth and degradation that seemed to plight my soul.

A.

I was glad to see the back of Mr Mason; the man was infuriating. He seems to ooze disdain for me not even having the grace to hide his disgust as he threw the key onto my desk. I admit tears formed in my eyes as I watched him leave. I feel pretty ashamed of myself. Why couldn't I have kept myself in check.

He made me feel so small and insignificant. Now as punishment for my childish behaviour, I was a day away from having to spend the whole weekend with him. The idea of being in his company under such testing circumstances was not something I was looking forward to.

I had no choice but to man up and accept his rejection and pretend yesterday never happened. The rest of the day seemed to drag, between phone calls and dictating letters I found I was breaking off into thought. The more I tried to keep him out of my mind the more I wallowed on the previous night's events. It's difficult to forget about someone when their voice echo's around your head. Listening to the tapes of his dictation I found nothing made its way into a letter I just sat and listened to his voice, even when the subject matter was the square footage of shipping containers his voice was still so powerful. It still stirred emotions in me that I had no right feeling. When I heard the door open, I assumed he had returned, but instead a woman stood in front of me holding the most beautiful flowers.

"Hello, can I help you?"

"Afternoon sweetheart, I have a delivery for Amanda Wake."

"Oh right. That's me, thank you."

I took the flowers and waited for her to leave before I took in the beautiful display. The smell was amazing. Every rose had a tiny jewel at its Centre. Who could they be from? James was the obvious answer, but I couldn't recall if I had told him where I worked? There was an envelope attached with my name on it.

I recognised the handwriting as Mr Masons, now my interest was piqued. I was a little afraid to open it, what if it was a polite form of handing me my notice? Taking a calming breath to steady my shredded nerves I opened it and read its content, then I read it again. Then again just to be sure I read it right on the previous occasions. Oh, my god, seriously Oh my fucking god.

I looked around the office just to help ground me, make me realise what I was reading was real. "He had feelings for me, he found me tempting", oh my god!

I had to get my beating heart in check I was only too aware that I was meeting James straight from work. We had planned on going for a pizza for an early dinner then on to catch a film. Titanic was out, and I had twisted his arm to watch it with me although he had protested and wanted to see G I Jane. All this seemed to pale into insignificance when I was faced with the contents of Matthews note.

Gathering up my bag and the large bouquet I left the office locking up as I went. I wanted to cancel with James, I wanted to go home and reflect on today's turn of events. I also needed to prepare for the weekend. Shit! The weekend! How was I meant to play this? It was all new to me.

Meeting James on the corner of Bridge Road I was a little taken back with his tirade of questions. Who were the flowers for? Who were they from? What for? I hadn't even though what his reaction might have been.

I was barely processing what it meant to me, let alone mine and James's relationship. Caught on the back foot I told him some truths, they were mine, and from Mr Mason, it was only seeing the anger and distrust in his face I was forced to think on my feet.

"They were sent as a thank you for staying late last week."

It didn't feel good to lie to him, but I knew what it meant. It meant I was making a choice. I was choosing to keep the developing relationship between myself and my new boss a secret. By keeping James in the dark, I was facilitating a lie. Laying the path to be a cheater should the opportunity arise.

If you ask me now what the film was about, I couldn't tell you I sat watching staring at the screen and none of the plot filtering through. My mind was elsewhere the whole night. After the film, James suggested we go back to his flat share.

I was so glad that I had an excuse to leave on the grounds of needing to pack for my trip. He was disappointed and a little pissed off, kissing me good bye; his passing words were that I should behave myself whilst I was away.

M.

Leaving the office, I used the car phone to make a call to the hotel. I needed to put some plans in place before our arrival. I made a point of telling them that Amanda was both a Diabetic and Gluten intolerant.

During our visit to the French restaurant she had been gluttonous with her approach to food, Fortunately, I was able to discourage her from eating dessert. However, I was quite sure she had undone all the work the laxatives had done. Checking our rooms were adjacent I was satisfied that things should run smoothly.

Returning home to an empty house I relished the silence. Mrs Mason was on some detox break, hugely expensive but worth every penny if it meant I had a few days' home alone to relax and prepare my mind. Even anticipating the weekend's events relaxed me I was looking forward to immersing myself with my obsession unrushed and uninterrupted. I ate alone listening to the rain as it pounded against the glass conservatory roof.

The shrill mobile ring broke my trance. Picking it up, at first I was surprised to see it was Amanda then I recalled I had programmed my number into her phone. Answering the phone, I waited for her to speak,

"Hello, Mr Mason?"

"Hello Amanda"

"Mr Mason are you okay to talk?"

"Yes, what's the problem? It's a little late Amanda shouldn't you be sleeping? We have a busy day ahead tomorrow."

"Yes, I just wanted to let you know I received the flowers, Mr Mason. I wanted to thank you."

"Good, did you like them?"

"Yes, they were beautiful it was very thoughtful of you",

I could tell from the tone in her voice she was waiting for me to take the lead, there were many pregnant pauses.

"Is there anything else I can do for you Amanda, it really is rather late?"

"Erm no Mr Mason that's all",

I decided to throw her a scrap, after all, I was suddenly feeling rather mischievous.

"I'm looking forward to seeing you tomorrow Amanda, sometimes the evenings seem so long, and I find I long for the morning to come back around so I can see you again."

"Oh ... the feelings mutual, Mr Mason, I don't know why but these last few days I can think of no one and nothing but you."

I knew she had feelings for me but for a moment I allowed myself to take it in, to believe that her words could be enough for me, closing my eyes just for a moment I accepted her declaration at face value. I actually wanted to whisper sweet nothings back, offer her wisps of love and affection. I really did try to say the right thing, but something about Amanda stopped me from being able to filter the real me. I found I couldn't offer her the comforting words she needed especially as in my mind all I could see was her spread leg and unconscious as I towered over her frail frame. Instantly erect at the memory I ended the conversation the only honest way I could,

"Get some sleep Amanda, I'm really looking forward to spending some time with you tomorrow".

I never waited for her response instead shutting the mobile and terminating the call.

Chapter 6

A.

Friday morning came around, and I made my way into the office, my overnight bag was small enough that I could travel by bus as usual. The morning went quite quickly. I had anticipated it dragging, but the calls were constant. Breaking for lunch at twelve I was surprised when the door opened, and Mr Mason stood at the door with two coffee cups in his hand, "Afternoon Amanda".

"Oh, hello Mr Mason I wasn't expecting you."

I could feel the blush creeping into my cheeks at an alarming rate as I desperately tried to control my erratic breathing.

"Amanda."

He took large strides towards my desk, taking my hand he helped me to stand."

"Look at you so flushed, don't threat child I won't bite, It's fine I just bought coffee, see?"

He offered the coffee cup up to me as a way of explanation

"I have the car outside I thought it would be easier if I drove you to the airport, that way we could go over my speech for the conference."

We closed the office up early and started on our way to the airport. If I had expected things to be difficult for us, they were not; I still firmly took the role of employee. The ninety minutes spent in the car was indeed dedicated to Mr Mason rehearsing his speech. He was word perfect from the get go however he insisted on going over it a further seven or eight times.

The rest of the journey was spent discussing which other companies would be at the conference and their relevance to us in the export game. Arriving at the airport we settled into the VIP lounge, champagne was the drink of choice, but I decided on Diet Coke, it wouldn't do to be drunk before we even boarded the plane.

The flight was quick we landed less than forty minutes after take-off. I had only flown on a few occasions, both times to Spain with my parents before mum had turfed dad out. The hotel was twenty minutes' drive from Edinburgh airport, we were met by a grand car, not being a car person I had no idea what it was but its interior smelt of leather and it had carpet floors plusher than in my house.

The hotel was a bit of a let-down in comparison. It seemed to be endless corridors of generic looking doors and carpets. It seemed clean enough and other than a small reception desk and a small bar its only redeeming feature was it had a partial view of Edinburgh castle. After checking in, we were directed to the fourth floor.

Our rooms were next door to each other. Mr Mason told me that we would be dining at the restaurant next to the hotel and that he would meet me at the bar at eight. It was almost seven, so that gave me an hour to get ready. Tonight's dinner was to be less formal than tomorrows so, after a quick shower, I settled on a newly purchased black pencil skirt and black blouse. Tying my hair back into a long plait. I applied my makeup carefully, going for a more natural look. Once I was happy with my appearance I slipped on a small pair of heels and made my way downstairs.

It was seven forty-five so. Fortunately, I was early, I ordered a large JD to help steady my nerves. The barman gave me a quizzing look before requesting my ID. Reaching for my purse, I once again thanked Dale. I sat sipping at my drink and waiting for Mr Mason to make his entrance. I had already composed myself in an effort to appear to be as unaffected by him as I could.

As I sat waiting a group of older men approached the bar. There was a distinct lack of women in this hotel by the looks of things. The group of men sat chatting amongst them self, but an older man about fifty caught my eye and winked suggestively. Not wanting to encourage him I looked away quickly and suddenly found the inside of my glass fascinating. Whilst I sat attempting to avoid eye contacts with dirty old men Mr Mason approached from my left. He must have left the hotel after we had arrived as the hotel residence entrance was on my right. "Hello Amanda, you are looking very sweet this evening, like butter wouldn't melt, can I get you another drink."

He actually winked at his own comment. This man was so confusing, so many mixed signals.

"Yes please, a double JD."

"Double? Take it easy Amanda we have a busy day tomorrow."

Realising I had exposed my nerves by displaying my need for Dutch courage, I decided he was right. Settling on a white wine instead. As we sat drinking Mr Mason introduced me to the group of man as acquaintances.

The sleazy older man confirmed my suspicions by making a show of kissing me on both cheeks whilst simultaneously groping at my arse. No one else seemed to notice, and I was a little too shocked to react. Instead of making a mental note not to get within groping reach of him again. Moving onto the restaurant I was pleasantly surprised it was fresh and modern. It was reassuring to see there were other women in attendance although we were the minority and they were all quite a bit older than me.

The wine was flowing as was the conversation. The man to my left introduced himself as Steve, he took the time to try to involve me in conversation, but it was difficult to follow as a lot of it went over my head. Mr Mason barely looked at me and seemed more interested in flirting with a middle-aged woman who was seated to his right. I found his nonchalant so frustrating I just wanted him to look at me. The food was nice although I Couldn't help noticing I had no bread roll with the soup starter, I don't care how posh a restaurant is, rolls should always be served with soup. I was a little disappointed with my desserts. Steve had a fantastic looking cake whilst I had a fruit salad.

I think I must have physically deflated when the waitress brought it to me as Steve suggested a swap. He was supposed to be on a diet anyway so was happy to have my fruit salad, the cake was amazing I would happily have had seconds. After dinner coffee was a little more bearable, the topics of conversation were more relatable to me, and I was happy to join in. Leaving the table to go to the toilet I realised the wine during dinner had been quite potent and my head felt a little fuzzy.

I took time in the bathroom to compose myself and re-plait my hair. Returning to the table, I saw the pervy man from earlier eyeing me up. I felt a shudder run through me as he seemed to run his eye over my barely there chest. The second set of eyes upon me were much more pleasing. Perhaps I was over analysing the look he gave me, but Mr Masons looked mirrored the pervy mans he was looking at me like he wanted to devour me.

Shortly after my return Mr Mason suggested we leave for the night as it had been a tiring day. I couldn't help but hope this was code for him needing to get me alone. I was drunk but not legless as Mr Mason directed me into my hotel room I refrained from throwing myself at him again instead perching on my bed trying to look as appealing as I could.

 He made no move towards me; instead, he went to the bathroom and brought back a glass of water and two pills to fight off any potential hangover. I took the water and pills and sadly wished him good night as he made his way back to his own room.

M.

Leaving Amanda's room, I pulled the door to gently making a point of not activating the lock mechanism. She has been iridescent tonight I had a real battle on my hands. The overwhelming urge to sit and watch her was all consuming. Instead, I found myself chatting to an old has been on my right. Allowing her to caress my leg under the table. It was her winking and suggestive looks that made me decide to cut our evening short. It was one thing flirting with her, but her wrinkly hand was making its way closer and closer to my crouch, and I didn't want to taint the up and coming evening with that memory.

 I went back to my room and waited fifteen minutes for the pills I had given Amanda to take effect. I was so eager to get back into her room those fifteen minutes felt like a lifetime. I paced my room, backwards and forwards, my whole body buzzing with anticipation. A constant clock watch was agonising. I needed to get back to her.

Somehow the last fifteen minutes had seemed like a lifetime. Stepping into the corridor, I checked left then right before going to her door. Knocking gently to see if she was still awake. When I got no response, I pushed the door open, I turned and locked the door from the inside. On the bed sleeping in the fetal position was Amanda; she looked so tiny lying there her eyelashes casting shadows across her cheeks. Her hair still plaited down her back.

I was eager to go to her to start what I had spent eighteen months planning, but first I needed to purge her of the fucking cake she had somehow managed to get hold off. Pulling her tiny body up into a seated position I had to force my fingers into her throat to encourage her to be sick, I had placed a bucket next to the bed and was pleased my aim was good, and it all went in. Now I had another problem if she had vomited up the cake it was likely she has also brought up the pills I had given her.

Fortunately for me, I had a syringe with a liquid form of the sedative in it. Taking off my belt I made a tourniquet around her arm. Her pale, bony arms offered up streaks of blue almost instantly. With a vain visible I injected her.

Now she was ready. Before lying her back down, I freed her hair from her plait. This was my time to unwrap my prize. Slowly and deliberately I undone the button on her night shirt. Peeling back her shirt, I was rewarded with two rosebud nipples. Lowering my mouth onto them, I was delighted when they stiffened in response. She was so beautiful. Lying so still and so quiet. I ran my tongue across her nipples and down her ribs towards her navel. Lying on her back as she was every one of her ribs were visible. I took my time licking over the bumps and bones that formed her beautiful rib cage.

I was more than delighted to see she wore simple white underwear. Her hips jutted up causing the fabric of her underwear to hover over her leaving a gap at its hem. I was pleased with how her body was looking my attention to detail had paid off; she looked so small and so frail. Positioning myself between her legs, I peeled her underwear off. I was presented with her golden curls a gap between her thighs displaying her sex for me to see. I was so hard my cock was throbbing for a release. But I wanted to take my time with her to enjoy the display on offer. Her skin was so beautifully pale.

Once she was naked, I laid on top of her bearing all my weight upon her tiny frame. She felt so warm. Her hips and shoulders digging into my body as I pressed into her. Taking my own clothes off I done the same again this time parting her thighs so she could cradle me between her legs. Her pubic bone protruded and pushed onto my cock causing a delicious sensation. As I lay cradled between her milky thighs, the weight of the world began to lift from my shoulders. Her breath brushed against my ear.

A soothing pattern of sleep, the only evidence she was alive. Her peace and serenity were soothing to my soul. I needed to penetrate her soon, my cock was engorged and painful. Breaking contact to put a condom on I felt cold and exposed. I longed to be back on top of her feeling her warmth and jagged edges. I wanted to savour this I wanted to take my time, but my own self-control was failing me. I should be able to do this, I needed this so why did my stupid body want to override my mind! Slapping at my face to centre my directive. Finally, I allowed myself to position myself at her entrance using my fingers to open her up for my invasion.

My excitement level was at ten, I heard panting, and it took a while to realise the noise was coming from me, Like an excited dog. Slowly and deliberately I entered her. I thought my memories of being with Amanda before may have been exaggerated over time, but it was better than I could ever have imagined.

No foreplay had ensured she wasn't ready for me she was so dry and so tight like a vacuum sucking me in. The sensation combined with her silence and lack of response had me ejaculating in short hot burst, her body was so delightful, she reduced me to a teenage boy again. Picking her up gently, remembering how frail she was I manipulated her onto her knees pushing her forward, so her beautiful pink arse was on display for me.

I had dreamt of this time. Burying my face between her none existent buttocks I tasted her at her very Centre, more than anything I wanted to take her here too but I knew I had to leave as little evidence as I could. I couldn't guarantee that presented with such an alluring opportunity that I could be gentle. I did, however, lie across her back taking in the dips and bumps of her protruding spine. The temptation was too much lying here with my still hard cock resting against her. In frustration, I flipped her over with very little ceremony plunging myself back into her more accommodating cunt.

I took my frustration out on her perhaps being rougher than I should have been, but there was no protest. Lifting her legs over my shoulders, I pounded harder and harder into her body. Her bony pelvis crashing into mine. My own sweat was dripping down my body. My panting breath and racing heart evidence of my strenuous activity, and still I did not slow my pace. If she was awake, she might have screamed out in pain asked me to stop.

The thought of this had me thrusting harder and deeper. Eager to own her body at all costs. Gripping at her beautiful silent face, I found my hands at her delicate neck enjoying the sensation as I gripped at it. So fucking small so fucking delicate. The orgasm that followed was phenomenally better than any drug or any high. Collapsing once again cradled between her thighs I welcomed the calm that washed over me.

A.

I woke up Saturday morning with a start the alarm on the bedside table whistling away. It must have been going off for a while I had set my alarm for eight, but it was eight twenty. Waiting a minute to ground myself I sat up gingerly.

The bed sheets were a little unkempt I must have had a restless night. Though I felt like I had slept like the dead. I made my way to the bathroom aware that the conference was due to start in less than an hour, brushing my teeth and barely giving myself a second glance in the mirror I checked on my clothes and made my way back to the restaurant for breakfast.

Mr Mason was already there he seemed to give me a disapproving look. Breakfast was pleasant although a little on the light side, more fruit for me by the looks of things.

 Half way through breakfast I excused myself and left for the bathroom. Whilst there, I couldn't help but notice I was a little tender in places I shouldn't have been. There seemed to be some dried blood in my underwear.

 This morning I had not done my usual blackout checks, I had full recollection of going back to my room. So how had this happened? Was my period due? I didn't think so. Sitting on the toilet, I noticed what looked like a start of a bruise on the inside of my thighs.

 I couldn't understand!? What could have happened? I had gone back to my room. Yes, I had been drinking, but I remember getting into bed. I recalled I was a little sad, another night of rejection from the elusive Mr Mason. But what had happened after that? Could I have got back up again perhaps, maybe drank some more?

Leaving the stool, I went and looked at my appearance in the mirror, I looked quite normal except for what seemed to be finger print marks forming on my neck. Confusion clouded my mind. Still unsure of the turn of events I walked back into the restaurant.

The first person I set eyes on was a Pervy man, raising his teacup as a salute, he winked. The thudding in my ears reminded me of the time I had fainted. Everything seemed to be moving in slow motion. Turning on my heels bile rising in my throat, I flew back into the bathroom just getting to the toilet in time to bring up my breakfast.

What the fuck had I done, was I really that desperate for attention I had got back up in search of anyone that would have me. I can only assume I had sought him out knowing he was a sure thing.

Any attention was good attention. He must have been rough; I was finding new bruises everywhere. Had it even been consensual? How could I prove it if it wasn't I couldn't remember a thing, Both Nell and Bella had said how much of a floozy I was when I was drunk. How I chucked myself at boys but would I really sink as low as to have sex with a fifty-year-old obese, balding man?

I had no choice I had to suck it up go back out and pretend I had no clue of what had gone on. Head down I scurried back to my table. I must have looked a fright as Mr Mason asked if I was okay, he said I looked as white as a ghost.

The rest of the day was a blur more than anything I longed to get back to my room and wash that dirty old man off my skin. I was so humiliated. I must have been so desperate. Getting back to the room that night I stood in the shower and washed away my sins. Everywhere was sore. I had planned on wearing a low-cut evening dress for tonight's dinner, I needed to be inventive with my make up if I was to disguise the bruises that had developed throughout the day. After going around and around in my own head, I was beginning to drive myself crazy, I decided to ring Bella. She would judge me, of course, she would, but maybe we could laugh about it make it seem more trivial. I needed to talk to someone. "Silly ole Mandy did it again, throws herself at anyone once she's had a skinful" I needed to hear a friendly voice, someone, to tell me I was going to be okay.

 Bella answered on the first ring. I never got the chance to tell her about my sins, she went straight into telling me about how Hollywood had been raided and how James and her brother had been arrested for supplying. Apparently, the copper that Dale had on the payroll had told them after he had no control over it.

 There had been a tip off, and orders to nick them had come from above. Of course, my news was pushed to the wayside as we discussed the possible ramifications for them both. I felt terrible for James he had a future planned, I wasn't sure if a criminal record would lend its self well to his intended career.

 I should have perhaps called him after speaking to Bella to offer some comforting words but decided that James may well be just the type of person I needed to avoid, Heartless I know but during that conversation, I had a flash of the life ahead of me, and it was my sister's life. A life I didn't want myself.

Sitting down at the vanity table I set to work disguising the various bruises that were appearing around my neck and collar bone. What kind of a monster was he? The evidence was there to suggest he had been anything but gentle.

 My whole body felt battered, as though I had been in an accident. Even sitting was uncomfortable, the bones in my arse seemed to be tender and bruised. Tears began to form in my eyes, I couldn't cry, I must not cry, I had a dinner to attend. The unshed tears burned in my throat as I applied foundation to my skin.

 The humiliation flooding my head with angry emotions. Why did I let this happen to me how could I not have been more careful? I had been in a black out before but always assumed self-preservation would save me from any compromising situations. Looking at my sorry state in the mirror I saw myself as others might see me. A push over someone who could be overpowered in a heartbeat. I have never felt as vulnerable as I did that night.

Sucking up the pain and sorrow that had plighted me all day I made my way down to the bar to meet Mr Mason. Head down refusing anyone the satisfaction of eye contact my body shook a little uncontrollably as I went.

M.

I sat at the bar and watch Amanda approaching, her head down her hair cascading down her back. As she took her seat in front of me, I noticed she was shaking a little her head darting left to right as if looking for someone that someone was not found as her tense body seemed to settle before my eyes. Her grey eyes were wet with unshed tears. Looking at me I could tell she was trying to maintain some kind of mask. A better man might have asked her what was wrong but sitting opposite me in that bar she looked so afraid, so frail and small. In short, she looked like a victim, and I found her demeanour unbelievably erotic.

Standing and adjusting myself to disguise my developing erection, I took her by the arm we walked towards the restaurant. To my delight, she ate very little that evening. Not so delightful she stuck to water. My plans for her were based on her teenage gung-ho approach to drinking, once she was inebriated, she was easier to control, easier to manipulate. She was quiet this evening preferring to sit with her hands in her lap instead of joining in the conversation.

I left the table on my return placing my hand on her shoulder; she almost jumped out of her seat she was so startled. Bending down I whispered into her ear

"Are you okay Amanda, you look as though you have seen a ghost?"

"Yes, I'm fine thank you."

"Are you sure, I can spot a lie when I see one Amanda, don't try to kid a kidder!"

She hesitated before she replied,

"Yes, I'm fine just a bit of bad news from home, my boyfriend has been arrested"

I was pleased with her response a few calls to the right people had got that cretin out of the way.

"I'm sorry to hear that Amanda, why don't you have some wine to drowned your sorrows?"

Shoving her hand over her glass

"No, no it's fine, thank you."

The eager protest had dislodged her silk scarf, as I helped it back onto her shoulders I saw the real reason for her distress, she had made an attempt to cover them but on her neck was a cluster of bruises. I must have been too rough with her yesterday evening the evidence apparent across her dainty neck. This was problematic, to say the least, I was hoping to enjoy her, and she never know, but now I could see that wasn't an option, changing my hand I needed to see if she recalled anything.

"Amanda, what is that on your neck "

"Erm ...sorry what?"

"You must know Amanda you have tried to cover them, they look like love bites of some description."

Turning to look at me she gave a slow well rehearse smile

"I'm sorry Mr Mason, how embarrassing, they are. I tried to cover them but as you can see I failed, my erm, my boyfriend is a little over zealous, I'm afraid."

How well she lies, how easily she thinks she can fool me, such a typical woman after all. Angry that the train of events meant that I was not to have a repeat performance tonight. I had to change my game if I wanted her before the weekend was over. Consensual was not something that peaked my interest but in this instance, it was all she could offer me. I was going to need to turn on the charm. Fortunately, she was susceptible to my advances. Running my finger across her shoulders, she mewed in response. Whispering in her ear

"Amanda, you look tired, my suggestion is we leave here and go back to your room for a night cap."

She seemed a little hesitant at first. Running my hand further down to the small of her back gave her the encouragement she needed. Tonight would have to be different if I wanted her in my bed I would have to do it her way.

I only hoped she wasn't vocal in the bedroom as I didn't want to plight the memory of the night before. Opening her bedroom door, I made a show of letting her go in first, now I needed to fall back on the expected courtship rules I needed to turn on the charm and woo her.

"You look very beautiful tonight Amanda; I have tried to stay away but am acutely aware of my need for you. Tonight might be our only chance to be together. If you would allow it, I would like to make love to you."

Of course, the silly little thing wanted me, she craved me more than she could ever possibly realise. I had been ingrained in her very being well before she had met me.

The sex was awkward and messy she was eager to try to please me, but her young age meant she was play-acting her way through the motions. Her body was still exquisite, but I much preferred it still and silent then fluid and in motion. She dropped her act once I made my way between her thighs. At first, she protested conscious of laying herself; so bear with me. I forgot she was only young her previous lovers were probably not as attentive to her needs as I was being.

I was pleasantly surprised that she only emitted small mews in response to her pleasure. Some women offer up shrill and blood curdling vulgar screams at the point of orgasm, all of which I find an intolerable endurance. Amanda instead gripped my shoulders gently with her small hands the only real evidence of her orgasm evident in the involuntary contraction of her muscles. Returning to intercourse, she tried her best to bring me to orgasm with her fruitless thrashing.

Knowing an orgasm wouldn't come, and with a condom to hide any evidence to the contrite, I faked a climax. Settling her to bed for the night I made her a hot chocolate to aid her sleep, before leaving her room.

Sweet nothings were offered up, and the appropriate distress was displayed that this was the first and last night that we could be intimate. Back in my room, I waited the twenty minutes for the liquid sedative to take control of Amanda's body.

Returning to her room, I enjoyed the silence I was met with. Now I was going to have her, my way. This silly little girl was just as disgusting to me conscious as all the other women I have had the misfortune to sleep with. Yet lying here now she was all I could have wanted all I needed. So beautiful and serene.

Fujifilm had just developed a new digital camera. They were expensive compared to the current cameras, but my expenses relating to Amanda seemed irrelevant. Buying it, I knew that it would bring me years of satisfaction. Taking time to pose her body I snapped away savouring the moment.

Positioning her to display her slender skeletal frame at its best angles. My own sexual excitement straining at my clothes. Eager for release I was deliberate and slow. Punishing myself by delaying my access to her. Once I tired of taking pictures, I stripped off all of my clothes. I wanted every part of me to touch every part of her. I wanted to smother her tiny body with mine. Entering her again this time I needn't fake it the orgasm it was as fulfilling and satisfying as it could be.

I knew my time with Amanda was coming to an end. The clarity of the risks I had taken was all too clear to me now. I had engaged in something she might consider a start of a relationship. The last thing I needed was a whining love sick eighteen-year-old trailing around after me. For the first time, I felt afraid, we were on the cusp of something real happening between us, something I couldn't maintain. It was so difficult to hide my true self with Amanda I couldn't risk exposing myself.

Before settling to bed for the night, I dictated a letter to the London office. I would ensure she had a job in the London branch if she wanted it, but her local office was relocating and me with it.

A.

I woke up before my alarm Sunday, the previous night's events milling through my head. I couldn't believe I had actually slept with my boss. I was surprised when he suggested we go back to my room. The more I thought about it, the more I wanted to. I needed to wipe the perves imprint from my body, and Mathew was the perfect person to do that for me.

I was surprised at the intensive feelings he stirred in me. Just placing his hand on my back had my head spinning. Going into my room had seemed like such a big step it was like making some big life altering decision. Once the door closed, he gathered me in his arms and kissed me. My knees actually weakened. I thought this was a feeling people only wrote about but standing in that room with this good-looking man I felt amazing, petrified of what was to come but excited in equal measures. What if I wasn't good enough, what if he was repulsed by me? Compared to his wife I was so scraggy and scrawny.

My heart was thumping faster than ever before. Pushing my doubts to the back of my head, I decided to enjoy tonight to relish the attention he was showering upon me. When he made love to me, I couldn't believe my luck. He seemed to know everything I wanted, touching me in places I had never been touched before. I didn't tell him, but he was the first person to ever bring me to orgasm. Now I knew what people wrote about there really were stars. I'm sure I even heard birds singing.

Today was a new day, and I felt amazing. I had wiped the slate clean burying the troubled weekend away I decided to embrace the future. With Mr Mason in it, it could only be bright.

Breakfast out the way I expected to spend the day with Mathew, I had hoped for a repeat performance. Tagging along beside him as we made our way back to the hotel I was upset when he didn't invite me into his room, instead suggesting some site seeing I might like to see before my flight home.

"We won't be flying back together Amanda, I have arranged a taxi for you I have some business to attend to so will be staying on",

I wondered why he was choosing to tell me this now, he must have known before today these were his plans.

"Oh, right erm... so when will you be back in the office?"

"I'm not sure Amanda."

How could he not be sure? What could have happened between last night and now to have him behaving so cold towards me? Last night he had been so warm so affectionate, He had lain with me our limbs entwined. Okay, he was telling me we had no future and couldn't be together again, but in the warm, after fuzz or our lovemaking, I had chosen not to hear his word.

I had assumed his efforts to stay away from me would be flawed. But looking at him now he was a closed book. The twinkle in his eyes had been replaced with a cold hard look. Reading his face, I could only describe him as dismissive. Was this really happening, had I been dismissed?

"Mr Mason ... Mathew, please!"

Closing the door with a curt nod that was our conversation terminated.

I'm not above spying choosing not to go sightseeing but to stay in my room instead with my ear pressed to our adjoining wall. I heard his door open fifteen minutes after our exchange. Giving him a few seconds to walk down the corridor so I could open my door undetected. Peering out I see the back of Mr Mason Black suit tailored to perfection, his overnight bag in hand looking very much like he was leaving to check out of the hotel.

With four hours before I was due at the airport, I sat in my room. Ears pricked for any sound that may have come from his room. My heart leapt with joy as I heard noises coming from his room a good hour after he had initially left. An hour of uncertainty and a continuing parade of scenarios going through my head had driven me slightly mad. Not above begging, I flew out of my room into his. Seeing his door was open and the commotion was in fact room services preparing his room for new occupants had me sliding down the wall and weeping into my lap. What had I done wrong, why had he just left me?

Explaining to a slightly confused Spanish maid why I had flung myself into the room she was cleaning and then fell to the floor in tears was not easy. Her grasp on English was not great, but eventually, she settled for the explanation I offered. Lost in translation, she had concluded I had been left by my father in the hotel room. By the time, I had explained it was not in fact, "home alone" episode I was feeling a little more composed.

Going back to my room and packing my case was a mundane experience but I immersed myself in it trying not to think about just how badly my Scottish soiree had panned out. Sure things couldn't get any worse I went and checked out.

Sitting in the taxi watching the city sights go by I'm hit with a terrible headache, sleep beckons, so I take a twenty-minute cat nap before I get to the airport. Rushing from the taxi, I almost forget the paperwork that the hotel receptionist gave me as I was leaving. A thick envelope catches my eye. It's another letter from Mathew. I'm filled with the same trepidation I had when he sent me the flowers, I can only hope that I'm wrong to be worried.

Opening the envelope, the first thing I notice is a wad of fifties there could easily be a thousand pounds' worth in there. Taking the letter out and securing the money back in my bag I sit in the airport and read what he has to say.

The airport swirls around me, the people in my peripheral vision. My mind is working on over time desperate to make sense of the nonsense that seems to be written before me. The Woofing branch of the office is to be closing with immediate effect. If I want to, I can relocate to the London branch. It is a much bigger operation, and there is room in the typing pool should I want to transfer.

There is no mention of the night we spent together no mention of any feeling he may have developed. Instead, a phone number for the coordinator of the head office details of possible flat shares in the area and that's it. No explanation for the money, nothing.

Heading home I don't know what to address first, how can I tell mum I have lost my job less than a month after I started it? James is also at the back of my mine, but I don't think I want to complicate the matter with him any further.

I made an ill-informed choice to cheat on him so couldn't see our relationship moving forward. Instead, I did what I do best I went to a bar and drank, I drank away the pain of rejection I drank away the pain of humiliation, I washed away all the sins that plighted me. I welcomed the darkness when it came engulfing me in nothingness.

M.

Leaving Amanda at the hotel had been the easy part, leaving a letter at reception was my coward's way of telling her I was done with her services. The harder part was excepting I needed to stay away from her.

The young, naive Amanda that worked for me as a typist was easy to leave, but the serene, beautiful child that had been entwined in my life for the last two years I struggled to walk away from. She had been my obsession for so long I wasn't sure what my next move was to be? I had spent so much time and money putting plan B in place.

My business head found it difficult to except that I needed to cut my loss after just three weeks. I had achieved my goal with Amanda I had the opportunity to immerse myself in her serenity, my soul did feel cleansed and fresh as a result, but how long would that last before I had to seek her out again. I made a decision to remove myself from Amanda's radar, but I knew in the back of my head I would need to see her again one day.

Part 2

Chapter 7

A.

Knocking back another shot I looked out to the sea. It was the second from last day of our honeymoon.

Tim was out on a surfboard laughing and waving to me as he tried to stay upright. The Bermuda sun prickling at my skin promising a killer tan for my return to London. Digging my feet into the sand, I was enjoying the sensation and the peace. It was only a matter of time before Tim tired of the surf and come bounding up the beach like a puppy looking for a scrap of attention.

Ours had been a short relationship no one was as surprised as me when he asked me to marry him, but I figured why not? It's better to regret something you did than something you didn't, right? We had met at a Madonna concert in Paris.

I had dragged both my teenage nieces along convincing them she was cool and could easily give Katy Perry a run for her money. He was there with his brother on his stag do. Not many people know where we met as he doesn't like to confess he was there let alone dressed in full "like a virgin" regalia. It was his voice that I noticed first not expecting to hear an English middle-class man singing away to borderline.

A tad younger than me at twenty-eight he was like my very own puppy dog from the get go. He says now he loved me at first sight. I can't say I felt the same to be honest he was handsome in a pretty boy kind of way, but my mandar had been switched off for a while, he peaked my interest, but there were no parting of the clouds and angels singing. We chatted and danced our way through the Madonna set. I had my nieces with me so had to go back to our hotel, and he had his stags to attend to, but we swapped numbers and agreed to meet up back in London. I'm the first to confess I don't let people in too easily. I have had a few relationships in my life, but I've yet to get my happy ever after.

A casual two-year relationship with Nate a work colleague had ended abruptly one Christmas. He was making his way back home after a Christmas night out with his friends when he was hit by a car. He was instantly killed; it was believed to be a drunk driver, but they were never caught. It was a while before I tried to meet anyone after that instead of locking myself away trying to come to terms with the grief that seemed to haunt me. After another night drunk on a friend's sofa, an old friend Bella decided enough was enough.

"Nobody is born a victim Mandy it really is time you dusted yourself off and lived your life."

So easy for her to say, but I had to admit it had been a lot of wallowing on my part. I was often plagued with depression feeling like the world was against me. Then one day out of the blue it was like a cloud was lifted.

At thirty most of my friends had paired up and long ago started their families. I lived alone in a one-bedroom flat. My days were busy with my career. I was successful in my field and content for a while to be immersed in it, but just lately I found myself wondering, what if. What if I could meet someone and start a family would it fill the void that I sometimes felt.

It was during one of these melancholy periods that Tim began vying for my attention.

He made me feel special, I liked to spend time with him. We got to know each other over the summer, and despite our different backgrounds, we got on well.

One good thing about contentment meant I finally gained some weight. I was beyond happy when I had to have my wedding dress made in a size eight. For years, I had battled to gain weight. My doctors eventually diagnosed me with irritable bowel syndrome. Years of unexplained bouts of stomach cramps and diarrhoea meant I never managed to get above a six.

I moved Tim into mine after three weeks a short time, but sometimes things just feel right. This was the first time I had lived with a man, and I liked it. Morning sex and breakfast in bed. Someone to watch television with in the evening. We shared a mutual appreciation of the pub, and I must admit I enjoyed knowing someone was there to see I got home safely after a heavy night. Barbeques on the roof terrace were fun, Tim would cook, and I would feast on new concoctions every weekend. Then feast on him at night.

I was enjoying being part of a couple I loved having someone to snuggle up to on summers evening. When he asked me to marry him, I decided to accept. Why couldn't I have a chance at happiness, after all, no one is born a victim?

The wedding was planned within three months. It was a pretty quiet ceremony neither of us having big families. The party after was in a nice bar close to our flat. I was far from a blushing bride and may have over indulged in the cosmopolitans. Tim was a little upset as he said I embarrassed myself in front of his parents.

As is often the case my memories are sparse. He forgave me soon enough and here we are now Bermuda sun shining down on the cusp of what I hope is our story.

"Hello gorgeous, you coming in for a surf?"

"Well my darling husband I believe I will, shall we race?"

Diving out of my chair I ran towards the sea as quickly as I could, of course, I didn't stand a chance his large athletic legs taking giant strides to catch me up. Picking me up above his head he threw me into the surf. Swimming back towards him and splashing water into his face I realised for the first time I truly loved this man

"I love you, Tim, I'm so excited about being your wife."

Grabbing me by the waist and pulling me in for a cuddle.

"I love you too Mandy, I love that you're my wife and I can't wait for you to have my children."

Plastering the smile on my face, I giggled as he spun me around in the sea. We hadn't discussed children before, but Tim was twenty-eight and newly married, why wouldn't he expect children to be the next logical step. I only hoped my luck held out because looking at him now drops of sea water resting on his lashes I wanted nothing more than to have his children.

Flying back into Gatwick that dreary October morning I held such promise in my heart. I was excited to be returning to the UK as Mrs March, it meant something to me, married meant I belonged to someone, someone had chosen me over everyone else. Looking a crossed at Tim's sleeping form I felt like one of the luckiest women alive.

My heart thawing for him in that Bermuda Sea had been a revelation for me. I know that as a rule, I shouldn't have married him if I wasn't sure I loved him but at the time I wasn't convinced I could love.

I had been in love only once before as a teenager. It was short-lived and brutal my heart was broken, I know I shouldn't have been so cynical I was young enough to pick myself up and dust myself off. I didn't shut myself of intentionally but no other relationship ever matched up in the feelings stakes. It had been a messy affair which almost destroyed me.

Almost eighteen and having thrown myself into a love affair with my older married boss I returned home from a trip to Scotland a wreck. The man I was convinced I was in love with had abandoned me. Returning to England, I blotted out my pain the only way I knew how with cheap cider and strong spirits.

Overnight I changed from a fun loving easy going teen into a drunken, thieving mess. I had no job to fund my excessive drinking instead, taking money from mum's purse whenever I could. I had been a well-behaved teen but waited until I was eighteen to go off the rails. Perhaps if it had happened when I was younger Mum may have been more forgiving.

My periods were never regular a result of being underweight, but after four months my mum marched me off to the doctors for a pregnancy test. Sixteen weeks pregnant with a choice of three fathers was a pretty sobering experience. Confessing to mum I wasn't sure who the father was, was enough to put the nail in the coffin of our failing relationship. I'm sure if Jeremy Karl was about in nineteen ninety-seven my mum would have marched me on there to expose my shame to the nation. Instead, she disowned me!

My own mother someone who should love, protect and cherish me abandoned me at my most vulnerable. To this day, it is something I could never forgive her for. I was confused love sick and broken not to mention expecting a child of my own.

I remember going to the abortion clinic, alone, this is something nobody should have to experience but who could I ask to go with me? Bella and Nell had made their opinions of me clear when I told them I had cheated on James sadly choosing his side over mine. I never did get to tell my story about the pervert in the Scottish hotel. Instead of pretending it was a young boy I had met whilst in Scotland. It's one thing confessing to being sexually promiscuous but admitting I was so drunk that someone abused me made me feel so dirty, so degraded.

Looking back, I was a victim that night, it shouldn't matter how drunk I was, no one had the right to take advantage of me the way that man had.

At sixteen weeks pregnant it wasn't just a case of taking a pill to terminate. They had to scan me to confirm dates, and I saw my child on the screen. I even made small talk expressing how grateful I was that I could still conceive after having an ectopic a few years before. What must they have thought of me! Stereotypical poor white trash. I carried that shame for so long.

It made me feel so worthless and undesirable. I couldn't love myself, how could I be expected to love someone else. Procedure complete I could only turn to my sister for my recuperation. She was my rock during that time, something I'm still truly grateful for.

Four and a half months after the Scotland trip I rang the number on the note Mr Mason had given me. Within the week, I had left home and was moving into a flatshare in Havering. Miraculously they hadn't found a flatmate during the time I had waited. A position in the typing pool at a sister business to the export company I had worked at before was offered to me. I worked my way through the ranks. Eventually becoming a buyer.

The rest I believe is history. Not an exciting story I know, but it's mine. Now finally after so long feeling so worthless and unworthy of love I feel I can embrace it. I decided now was my time. I was going to drown myself in the depths of my husband's devotion. Happier than I thought I could ever be. With the prospect of having a family on the horizon, I felt like I could finally put the sins of my teenage mistakes behind me.

M.

After Scotland, I travelled, moving as far away from Amanda as I could. Convincing myself, I didn't need her anymore. Replicating her to achieve physical release, a business trip to Thailand, young girls were everywhere whenever the urge took me, there was no shame on my part in requesting their silence, asking them to keep still as I thrust away. Some of them were so high I didn't even ask them to act the part for me, they would simply lie there and accept my body.

The physical releases came easily, but my mind remained chaotic. I prided myself on needing no one, but some nights as I buried myself in a conveyer belt of girls I missed her. I miss being able to watch her through the fish-eyed lenses I had on her computer.

I missed the diary entries exposing her childish mind. Returning to England, I was faced with new challenges. The troll had decided it was time we started a family, it was the one thing now apparently, all the rage. Like a new handbag, she wanted it, so I was expected to comply.

I had a pleasant surprise when I got a call from my source, Amanda had made contact. She had waited almost five months but had finally taken up my job offer. More importantly, she had plans to move into the room I had set aside for her.

The first night she spent in her new room I chose to spend at a hotel. I knew if I stayed at home with the troll I would not be able to disguise my nerves. So eager to see her again I sat in my hotel room surveillance gear at the ready, seeing her on the small grainy screen for the first time in five months I had a whole wave of unfamiliar emotions flowing through me.

The overwhelming feeling was that I was finally back home. I hated that I needed Amanda, I hated that I couldn't replicate the calm and serenity she gifted me with. Even not knowing I was there watching her, her actions seemed to be for my pleasure. I refused to become embroiled in her life again. So afraid of the realisation she stirred emotions in me, emotions I had no right feeling. So, I watched her instead. I watched her in her room, and I watched her at her desk, I had access to her emails and even had her office phone bugged.

Owning the building, she bunked in meant I would go to her room when I knew it was empty. I was able to maintain a control on her body. Injecting liquid laxatives into her daily yoghurts. On the harder days, the days when the noise and traffic and smells of the city overwhelmed me I would crawl into her unmade bed and breathe her in, closing my eyes against the chaos that threatened to consume me I would seek comfort from knowing she would be lying in the same bed that night.

It was by far my favourite pass time. Over the years, I was almost content. Juggling my home life which was almost bearable now, the troll despite her faults had birthed me a son. He was a bundle of laughter and joy, He mellowed the troll too, to an almost tolerable level and with him in my life I made the best effort I could to be a good father. I found I could watch her less, combined with a string of no complicated liaisons with paid whore's I could juggle my coping mechanism alongside "normal" life.

Unfortunately for Amanda, my relationship with the troll came to an abrupt halt around two thousand, taking my son she moved away. I never missed her for a moment, but by taking my son, she had taken one of the only things that grounded me. I compensated by throwing myself back into my go to stress release.

Amanda soothed my soul. Her daily emails were my reading material of choice. I was proud of the women she had become, Proud of her career progression. She might not be aware that I was still her employer, but that was irrelevant her progress and promotions were out of my hands. The only liberty I took once she was moved to her own office was to have a coffee machine fitted in her room. A coffee machine which had been tampered with to aid her weight loss. But otherwise, my lack of involvement in her career advancement meant it was all down to her. Her emails become a little troubling when she started corresponding with a colleague. Flirty emails turned into cosy chats on the phone, and before long he was also showing on my grainy CCTV images.

I felt envious watching him making love to her but not as much as I felt turned on, watching them was so satisfying the only downfall was the footage was poor. I made a point of updating the equipment the next time I went to the flat. I was happy to tolerate Amanda's and Nates relationship getting my own kicks from watching him fuck her the way I longed to. Some nights I would watch her falling through the door too drunk to stand as I would watch him put her to bed and leave the perfect gentlemen.

Except for one night, around Christmas. She had been drinking in the office, and I assume they had gone to a pub. Returning to her room he put her to bed as always. But once she was soundly sleeping he went to her. Removing her clothes, he seemed to be taking pictures of her with his phone. I'm the first to admit it made me horny as hell. I had my cock in my hand in an instant. Stroking myself as I watched him taking snap after snap.

The irony not lost on me. By me watching him the hunter was being hunted, that night he signed his fate.

It's only now I question my motives, why did I have to kill him? We don't often kill for like, we don't kill for disdain, but we do kill for love and hate. Both were the same to me.

Did I love her? Could I love her? Surely not, even I knew that this was far from a conventional love story!

I followed Nate two nights after, feeling more manic than usual. I was in a rental car following him at a slow pace. The radio playing Christmas songs in the background. I didn't have a plan I just knew I had to act. I followed at a good distance so as not to arouse suspicion. Entering a residential area. The road was quiet the Christmas revellers sticking to the main road. He crossed the road up ahead. Seeing an opportunity, I pushed down on the accelerator.

I could hear a giggle, at first assuming it was the radio, but it was me like a child giggling away in anticipation. He didn't see me coming too consumed with the music on his headphones. The car hit him at fifty miles an hour. His head bulls-eyed the windscreen. His body bounced from the windshield and into the road.

Slowing the car down me climbed from the car. Nervous eyes scanning for any witnesses. His crumpled body lie on the floor at an unnatural angle. I knew he was dead his brain matter was on the floor. Checking again that we were alone

I Reached into his pocket and took what was rightfully mine. The phone with the photographs.

Watching her on the screen tears flowing and heartbreaking I had to fight the urge to go to her. Not to comfort her. I was not that kind of man, but to bury myself in her sorrow and ease my own pain whilst doing so. Watching her weeping fragile body displayed on my screen was the only thing that stopped me approaching her again, the satisfaction I got from seeing her so frail and broken was immense.

I credit her sorrow and despair for helping me through many lonely nights. I was saddened once she seemed to perk up saddened that I was no longer able to watch her wallowing and pity. Somehow in front of my eyes, she seemed to grow stronger the sorrow was no longer visible on her face. She had gained strength from someone or somewhere.

There are many perks to being the boss, but ultimately Amanda had a manager that oversaw her. It was too big a corporation for me to have a handle on every employee. I assume therefore I never found out until it was too late that Amanda had left us. Apparently, she had been head hunted and immediately placed on gardening leave.

This is a self-preservation policy for most companies, especially so if there is a danger of clients being stolen by previous employees. After a particularly tiring week I was eager to unwind and chose my usual method of monitoring Amanda, it was only once I tried to access her emails and see her account had been suspended that I was alerted to her absence. In a frenzy, I turned to the spy wear in her room desperate to see her.

Her room was empty everything boxed up or removed. It seemed that she was moving on in more ways than one. To say I was frantic is an understatement. Where was she? I know a lot of shady characters and have method and means to find out any information I require, but it seemed the trail was cold. Surely her new company would require a reference of some description; no contact was made.

For the first time in a long time, I suddenly felt afraid. Almost fifteen years Amanda had been part of me, part of my coping mechanism. She was the one thing that grounded me when the whole world was spinning too fast. My behaviour was erratic as a result I perhaps was less careful than I should have been. Exposing my true nature. I dealt with her loss by approaching a young girl who bore a striking resemblance to Amanda except she was young, very young.

A person like me does not have a conscience as a rule, but I did feel some pity when I realised the physical harm I had caused the young girl. She was not ready for me to use her the way I did. Her body not yet able to accommodate the wants of men.

Fuck Amanda! She would be my downfall! If I couldn't find her I was really in danger of exposing myself as the monster I knew I could be.

I'm not proud of the depths I sunk into in an effort to forget Amanda, but I tried to conduct most of my less savoury acts outside of the country. She had been gone so long now I have long ago lost hope of seeing her again.

Standing at the airport conveyer belt at Gatwick, another "business trip" to replicate the serenity I have only ever found with Amanda.

The hair on my arms suddenly stands on end. It's cool in the reclaim lounge, but I am suitably dressed in shirt and blazer. My heart starts to quicken; my heart beat suddenly deafening in my ears. The world seems to be moving in slow motion. Looking around I look for something to ground myself with, Then I see her.

Older and carrying more weight. Looking tanned and incredibly happy I see Amanda. I must resist the urge to throw myself at her feet. My goddess my saviour, after three long years she is here in front of me completely unaware of the turmoil her absence has caused me.

Beside her is a large man, they are walking arm in arm. She catches my eye, and I see the recognition on her face see her take me in and a thousand emotions seem to be displayed in her beautiful grey eyes. She has stopped dead and is watching me watch her.

The baboon next to her interrupts our beautiful reunion by speaking

"You okay Man, you look like you have seen a ghost?"

"Yes, fine just seen an old friend, come I will introduce you."

"Mr Mason, long time no see, very good to see you."

"Amanda."

It's the best I can offer her now as I'm aware that my voice is small and broken, portraying the emotions that are bubbling away beneath the surface.

"How have you been Mr Mason, you are looking well, hardly aged a day, and how long has it been"

I want to say thirteen years four months two weeks.

"Almost fifteen years, too long Amanda",

I take her warm, delicate hand in mine and stare into her eyes. As if remembering her partner, she moves to the left to introduce him.

"Erm Mr Mason, this is Tim March, my Husband, Tim this is Mr Mason my very first boss."

Pleasantries are exchanged, I try to be civil, but internally I'm in turmoil. Husband? How did I let this happen, she was mine damn it, nobody else had any right staking claim to her!

"good to meet you mate, Man our bags coming let's grab it and get back, if we hurry we will be back in time I can run you a nice bath, if you play your cards right I might join you in it."

Winking at me just to emphasise his ownership he steers her away from me.

I should follow; I should see where she goes, but my legs don't feel like they belong to me. I have no fight in me. Instead, I sit, I hang my head low and try to reclaim my heart beat.

A.

Leaving the airport, I'm still a little light headed. I love Tim to the end of the earth and back but seeing Mathew standing there, looking so gorgeous it was like the last thirteen years had never happened, I'm reverted to being seventeen and star struck. Back to being in his bed amazed that such a magnetic, charismatic man would want to be with me.

Trying not to alert Tim to my internal dialogue I Fein sleep once we get in the car, giving me the opportunity to evaluate the feelings seeing Mathew has stirred. Newly married to a darling of a man yet seeing Mathew has stirred feelings I never thought it was possible to feel again. Of course, I recall how I felt for him but the passing years have convinced me it was a teenage obsession and it was time itself that had magnified them feelings to unrealistic proportions.

The reality is I barely know him a brief infatuation does not make a lifelong love affair; however, my treacherous heart is saying otherwise. I feel genuinely gutted a sense of grief is coming over me. My heart feels like it has been broken all over again.

Fortunately, sleep becomes my real saviour, and I managed to have a restless dreamless sleep before we arrive back at the flat. I wake all too aware that I should be ecstatic, happy that I have finally been dealt a good hand. Sucking up my feelings of sorrow I try my best to cheer up. It's made easier as Tim scoops me up in his strong arms and proceeds to carry me across the thresh hold.

"Now for that soak in the bath Mrs."

He looks at me so loving and so sincere my heart melts a little more. Tim goes running a bubble bath whilst I make us some coffee. Manhandling me into the bathroom my new husband kisses me into a beautiful breathless frenzy.

Peeling off our clothes we sink into the bubbles. As Tim caresses me, he looks into my eyes.

"You are so beautiful my darling wife, I'm such a lucky man."

I can feel his erection pressing against me and squirm against him in response. Opening me up and whispering into my ear as he does

"Mandy, I'm not wearing a condom, is this okay?"

He thrust up slightly just enough that he barely enters me. I nod my approval, and he enters me with enthusiastic groans. I guess this was when the baby making was first attempted. The day we returned from our honeymoon skin sun-kissed and warm. The smell of vanilla bubble bath in the air. Two people whose body united in pleasure to attempt to create a new life. Enjoying the physical sensation my husband never fails to highlight in me, I have one overwhelming thought, Mathew.

Two days after the end of our honeymoon I had to return to work. My colleagues asked the obligatory questions and ooohed and arhed in the right places. I was glad once lunchtime came. I was meeting Lucy. We had worked together for a few years and had developed a close relationship. She was bright and bubbly, A gazelle of women all legs and tiny waist. Full of exciting stories and funny tails. In short, she was everything I wasn't.

I loved spending time with her she brought out the louder braver version of me.

We met as we always do, in a pub. Lunch would be of the liquid variety. Hugging Lucy as I met her at our usual table.

"Mandy, that tan is to die for darling you look amazeballs."

"Cheers, weather was beautiful, I managed to spend my days lounging in a sunbed cocktail in hand, pure bliss."

"Ah don't I'm so jealous, I have another three months before I go away I am so pale I'm positively transparent. So, spill we only have.... fifty-three minutes before we are due back in the office, how was it?"

"Well, the condensed version is, got on the plane got off the plane, sunbathed, swam in the sea, drank copious amounts of alcohol and decided to try for a baby."

Lucy looked me in the eye swallowing her g and T,

"A baby?"

"Yep, a baby."

"I didn't know you wanted kids Mandy."

"Well I've never not wanted them if that makes sense, just the time has never been right. I've never been in the position to actually have to really consider it."

"Are you in that position now? You barely know Tim, how long have you been together seven months?"

"Hmm hmm, but I've married him, Luce, that's not something that you do for a laugh, its real commitment, till death do us part. Plus, I love him, I do love him, I want to give him a child."

"Then great, if you're good with it then so am I."

We hugged it out Lucy giving a high-pitched giggle and rubbing at my flat tummy.

"Just think Mandy you're going to be a mum!"

"I know I'm really nervous Lucy, but above all else I'm excited, I think I'm ready for this, we should celebrate!"

Two Jager's later we wobbled our way back to the office.

Tim met me at work today we went for a curry and a bottle of red.

"How was your day babe, you look knackered."

"Good thanks, Lucy and I had a pub lunch."

"Ahh that explains a lot, liquid lunch, was it?"

He looked at me a little disapprovingly.

"Yes, it was"

"So, you're probably not tired then just half cut?"

"that would be correct husband dearest, don't look so disapproving, though, the red wine has managed to paint you in the sexiest light and is giving me the courage to tell you I think you should take me to the toilets for a ration of passion."

The disapproving look was now replaced with a knowing smile and a twinkle in his eye.

"A ration of passion, aye? Who even says that anymore Mandy? Tell you what ask me again nicely, and I might consider it. Try being a bit more explicit with your requests too you know I like your mouth dirty."

Looking him square in the eye and licking my lips in what I was hoping was a seductive manner.

"Tim, would you please take me to the toilet so you can fuck me over the sink?"

I felt the heat rising in my cheeks but maintained eye contact long enough to see his face crack into a smile, putting my hand in his we moved towards the disabled toilets as discreetly as we could.

On the tube journey home, the wine and excitement got the better of me, I rested my head on Tim's arm and had a power nap. Once again grateful that my husband and protector were there to watch over me whilst I slept.

Chapter 8

M.

It had been two weeks since I had seen Amanda at the airport. I hate to admit it but seeing her had knocked me for six. So much so I had become unwell. Sitting in the baggage reclaim, I found I was sliding off my chair to the floor. My mouth full of a metallic taste and an overwhelming pain in my left arm, at first I was disorientated not understanding what was happening.

A crowd formed around me, and my vision began to close in. Lying on that floor with a Millard of people fussing around me.

Some people say your life flashes before your eye at such times but not me. As I lie on that cold floor under the bright clinical airport lights I had one thought, one aim, try to find Amanda in the crowd, from my view point I could see only legs and feet and yet I searched. I only stopped searching when the blackness took over, and I lost consciousness.

I'm a few days off being discharged. It seems at fifty-one, I had my first heart attack. Fortunately, not too serious but a combination of a private hospital and having no one to go home to meant I had been kept in longer than was necessary.

For the first time in my fifty-one years I actually felt vulnerable, I felt weak. I accepted the care given in the private clinic, for a while I was content to be the patient, to be less able than those around me.

As I become stronger, I battled with my own mortality. A man of my stature rarely wants or needs for anything. Not much is beyond my control, yet here I was struck down and broken. Worst of all it was seeing Amanda that had done this to me. The person who I go to when I need control and stability had unwittingly caused me to completely lose it.

Whilst the moments before my heart attack were filled with thoughts of Amanda, the recuperation was time for me to evaluate my life so far. I am a very successful businessman. I have numerous properties scattered a crossed the globe, and although I have no interest in cars, I always have the most up to date top of the range vehicle. My ex-wife was considered by most to be at the top of her game. Many men and women found her to be attractive. I wear made to measure suits and have the finest watches.

On paper, I had all that a man could ask for, yet my health chose now to fail me. I'm not an unfit man granted I don't go to the gym often, but I eat healthily and maintain my weight by swimming, regular golf meant I do plenty of walking and get lots of fresh air, my alcohol intake is minimal, and I don't smoke. Yet my arteries saw fit to clog up on me and try to terminate my life. I can't help but ask myself why? Why me? Why now?

It takes these questions and hours of time on my hands, sitting and mulling things over. I have concluded that the only vice that could have caused my ill health is Amanda. But a vice is a bad thing surely? So why is Amanda bad for me? More importantly, if I can acknowledge she is bad for me why can't I find the willpower to rid myself of her negative impact? Why still now as I lie in my hospital bed angered that the treacherous bitch went off and got married. Why do I still have the urge to seek her out?

I no longer want to wrap myself in her sheets to get comfort from her smell. I'm now in a position where I need to. I need to be close to her to calm my breaking heart. I'm not sure I can watch her from the shadows anymore. I think the time is near where I must claim her, she is the only medication I need. Her still silent body soothes my soul. She is my true addiction, and I'm now certain she will be my downfall.

I'm a little apprehensive that I won't be able to find her. The meet at the airport is all I have to go on. Whilst it pained me at the time I'm grateful she introduced me to her baboon of a husband, with his name I have more of a chance of finding him.

Once I find him, she will follow closely behind. It's so much easier to find people nowadays with social media at everyone's fingertips. A Google search for Tim March brings a few interesting leads. I hit the jackpot when I find a Facebook link. The profile picture shows a thumbnail picture of a bridal couple. Clicking on it I'm greeted with Amanda and her new husband. His profile is private, but I do have some information to go on, he was tagged in a few pictures playing rugby for a club an hour's drive from my London office.

I will need to be clever, I can't just turn up at a rugby match expecting to find her. I need to be in this for the long game. I'm mauling a plan over when I notice in another picture the sponsor is displayed on Tim's Rugby shirt. Bingo, the sponsor, is a business acquaintance I'm sure with a few calls put in the right place I can bag an invite to the next game.

Alone in my hospital bed, I'm feeling pleased with my progress for the first time in almost five years Amanda is back within my grasp. Content my work is done for the day I decide to remind myself what it is about Amanda I find so alluring. Digital Cameras a thing of my past I'm glad I had the foresight to save my most important pictures to a file on my laptop. The quality is poor the lighting bad, but the Scottish images provoke the emotions in me I want. They take me back to the night when she slept so soundly and serene as I violated her tender seventeen-year-old body. So small and fragile.

I will have my work cut out getting her back to her former glory and tiny weight, but I'm prepared to do it. Looking at the images of her laid bare for my eyes only I feel a flicker of sexual excitement. Reaching down into my shorts I only hope my ticker holds out.

A.

Honeymoon well and truly a thing of the past I am fighting my way through the London underground. I have a doctor's appointment before work so left a little later than usual which meant my normal train has been replaced with a train full of school children on their way to school. Standing in the carriage I've had the pleasure of listening to how Britney

"Is barely done with Shane now, he liked some slags insta enit"

And how Candy

"Ain't doing no homework Mrs Neive can just do one, as my mum said I don't have to do it as I ain't never gonna go France anyway."

Worst of all I cringe a little as its still fresh in my mind that I was one of these girls not so long ago. Being a teenager at such a difficult time, eager to fit in and seem cool. For a while, I was a bit off the rails, but it was moving away that gave me a clearer perspective. Not everything revolves around the local park and a tin of TNT cider, but when you're fourteen and all your friends are drinking and snogging boys sometimes going with the flow is the way forward. I had my downfall, I was pretty unlucky as a result of some stupid teenage mistakes.

One ectopic and an abortion later. I'm finding these events are fresh in my mind now I'm trying for a baby. I know it's ridiculously early to stress we have only been trying a few weeks but I have booked the doctor's appointment to talk things over. I want to go into this as healthy as I can. Hoping my past mistakes won't come back to haunt me.

Arriving at the Doctors, I'm met with a beast of a receptionist barely looking up long enough to acknowledge me before ranting at a rather timid-looking man next to me that "if he wants a repeat prescription he needs to write it down and come back in forty-eight hours."

When I finally get called into the surgery a full half hour after my appointment time I see a doctor I haven't seen before.

"Hello, Mrs March what can I do for you today?"

"Hello DR, I and my husband have just started to try for a baby I just wanted a MOT if possible make sure I'm as fit as I can be, I also have a few questions. I had an ectopic pregnancy when I was quite young, I assumed my fertility would have been compromised, but I fell again a few years after. I just need to talk it over with someone to see where I stand?" the doctor lowered their glasses, looking across the frames at me

"It is understandable you should be worried, did you have a laparoscopy?"

Met with my blank look, she rephrased,

"Did you have your fallopian tube removed?"

"Erm yes, I assume so, I definitely had surgery I have a few small scars."

"Right but you went on to have a healthy pregnancy and baby, when fallopian tubes are removed the second ovary tends to compensate for the loss and fertility isn't often affected."

I felt the need to correct the doctor, trying hard not to portray my shame

"Erm no I didn't go on to have a baby."

Saying this out loud caused my face to redden the heat on my neck evident, it was a conversation I had only ever had with my mother.

"I was quite young, so I opted for an abortion."

If the doctor was judgmental, she gave nothing away.

"Are your periods regular Mrs March?"

"Yes, they are now, they have been irregular, I have IBS, and for a few years I struggled to gain weight which meant my periods were a bit erratic, but they are better now."

"Okay well I will do a blood test just to check all your levels are okay, I'm going to prescribe some pregnancy vitamins, and as long as you eat well and cut out smoking and drinking, I think you should be fine to conceive."

"Thank you, doctor, that's such a relief, thank you for your time."

Taking the form for the blood test and the prescription for folic acid I floated out of the doctor's surgery. I hadn't realised how heavily it had been playing on my mind. I didn't want to express my concern to Tim, my past was something I decided not to share with him. I had been judged enough by my own mother I didn't want him thinking badly of me as well.

The blood test was done swiftly and relatively painlessly, I made my way to the office stopping off for some coffee and a muffin on the way. It was the middle of October; the days were getting colder it wouldn't be long before the clocks went back. Feeling the chill in the air, I decided on an Irish coffee to keep the chill at bay.

The office was quiet I kept busy going over old invoices and checking off unanswered emails. Instead of dictating letters I decided to type them up myself. Falling back on my typing roots. At lunch Lucy and I did some window shopping, stopping a tad too long to consider a shop window of pushchairs displays

"Come on Mandy, you will have plenty of time for that once baby is on board, if we hurry we will get to Debenhams, and they have a shoe sale chop."

"I'm coming, but do you really need more shoes?"

"Mandy!?, are you even a real girl??, check your pants for a penis. No women ever asked that question. Women, always I repeat always need more shoes."

Laughing at Lucy, I picked up my pace to catch up so we could make it to the shoe sale and back in our lunch hour.

"Oh, my god, Mandy look at these aren't they gorgeous and they are reduced to thirty quid!"

In her hand, Lucy was holding a pair of high heels the likes of which I would fall over in as soon as look at. They were beautiful though even a shoe phobic such as myself could appreciate their beauty.

"you should try them on Luce, look that kids balloon had floated up I reckon with them on you could reach up and get it for him" "ha bloody ha, piss off shorty!"

She did try them on and whilst she didn't quite reach the ceiling they extenuated her long legs to supermodel proportions.

"They are nice Lucy, you should buy them, they might help you pull, I think you're in need of some help your face must be scaring the blokes away."

Of course, this couldn't be further from the truth she was stunning, but she was still single mostly because she was fussy.

"Mandy I need your help you need to set me up with one of them scrummy rugby boy Tim plays with. I'm still gutted all his brothers have been married off".

"Ooh that reminds me, Lucy, a few weekends from now there is a match and a charity auction thing, Tim asked me to ask you, but it slipped my mind. Fancy do black tie. Do you fancy it?"

"Will it be full of rugby players Mandy?"

"Well yeah, of course, plus a few corporates I reckon."

"Well, I suppose me and my new shoes can make it."

"Brilliant you can stay over at ours after I'm looking forward to it, now come on we better get back to the day job".

Chapter 9

M.

Home from the hospital I was a little disappointed at my slow recovery, I found I tired easily and was sleeping more often. I eased myself back into exercise. I needed to get my strength back I had plans I wanted to put into action. Living the life, I choose is often a balancing act.

I was acutely aware of my need to re-establish my relationship with Amanda, I was convinced now more than ever that she was the cure to my damaged heart only she could offer the serenity I needed to restore my soiled soul back to the clean slate I needed to maintain some kind of normality. Secondly and less importantly I needed to restore normal facade. Since the Bitch had up and left there had been no other public significant other, I needed to maintain "normal" I had an image to portray.

This was a much harder task because this was a little out of my hands. I would need to meet someone who I could convince I was interested in someone who could play wifey. I knew there was enough money grabbing bitches out there looking to line their own pockets that finding a suitor would be easy enough it was the time and trouble I would have to invest in keeping her.

Fortunately, things had changed a lot since I had last decided to find a partner. There were dating apps and site for that now. That should cut out some of the painful encounters I had experienced in the past. Where nasty trashy women threw themselves at me to secure a night in a fancy hotel. I was a meal ticket, I knew that, why not advertise myself as one that way there was no confusion. Except a lot of these women wanted to exchange sex for the high life, they were whores by another name.

If only there was a website with a no sex clause, the last thing I wanted to do was find myself with no choice but to fuck someone to placate some whining whore. Leaving the house for the first time since I had been unwell, I decided to take it slow.

A day of light duties followed, I had a haircut and a close shave. My hair had always been wayward, first marking me out as different with my mallard's streak, it was also thick to a fault. I had hoped with age it might have thinned a bit, but it was showing no sign yet. Once my hair had been cut I had a light lunch and purchased a few jumpers.

The weather was turning and whilst I wore suits through the week I like a jumper at the weekends especially if I was playing golf. Enjoying the fresh air, I didn't want to rush back home, but there is only so much shopping a man could tolerate. Sitting on a bench in the shopping Centre I opted for a bit of people watching instead.

 A gaggle of girls barely sixteen walked past giggling amongst themselves. Reminding me of the time I followed Amanda home. Looking at them so innocent and pure I must admit my interest was peaked. A smaller younger looking girl with dark hair caught my attention. I was suddenly acutely aware of what I was becoming, a fifty-one-year-old man dribbling over young girls in a shopping Centre. There was a name for men like me, I was best not to draw attention to myself because if any digging was done, there was plenty of evidence to back up my unlawful attraction.

The sooner I got my cover girlfriend the better. I was becoming a cliché. Picking up my bags I made my way to a bar. It was empty, but it was less likely my eye would be drawn to barely pubescent jail bait.

A.

It was the morning of the charity dinner; I had woken up a grouchy bitch. Tim had a game at one which I was expected to go and watch then home, dressed and out to dinner. Going to the bathroom I was confronted with the reason for my fail mood, my period had come. It was actually a few days late. This isn't rare as I'm often irregular but still, in the back of my mind I had allowed myself to hope just a little bit, hoping it might mean we had fallen pregnant.

 I actually felt a little sad if I'm honest. I know we had only been trying a few months and often couples must try for ages before it happens, still, in the back of my mind I was hoping it would happen quickly, it seems we spend most of our youth trying not to. It's drummed into us that as soon as look at a willy twins are on the way. Yet here I was a thirty having done a lot more than look at one and failing miserably. Oh, well there was always next month.

 It would mean I would have to change my wardrobe choice now, though, I had planned on wearing a beautiful white dress, now I would have to dig through my wardrobe for a something a bit darker should the unimaginable happen.

Leaving the bathroom, I was met with the unmistakable smell of bacon, Tim was in the kitchen whistling away.

"Good morning beautiful, do u want a sandwich."

"Yes please, can you make my bacon crispy?"

"Of course, anything for you, my love,"

He said this accompanied by a brief bow and a cheeky smile. Sitting at the breakfast stool, I watched Tim cooking for me and felt grateful. So, what our baby making plans weren't going quite to plan, we were enjoying trying, and I was enjoying life. I felt I needed to tell him about my period, though. I wasn't sure what time scale he had put on things if any? Had he expected a baby just to magically appear?

"Do you want sauce on your bacon Mandy?"

"No thanks."

"What's wrong why you looking so sad?"

it often amazed me just how attuned to my moods Tim could be, yet at other times I could just as easily send a smoke signal then have him pick up on a mood,

"Ahh not much, just I got my period today, just a little sad that's all."

The hormone that comes attached to periods go the better of me at this point, and the tears began to fall. Big fat salty tears. I wasn't even sure if I was crying because I had my period or I just had an overwhelming sadness that decided to escape through my eyes.

"Oh, Mandy don't cry sweetheart its only early days, come here."

With that, he opened his big bear arms, and I found my happy place snuggled up against his chest. Through sobs, I managed a garbled apology about not being a fruitcake and my emotions getting the better of me. Fortunately, my husband knew me well enough that he fixed me with bacon and coffee.

After regaining control of my wayward emotions, I explained my predicament about not being able to wear the dress I wanted to wear. Tim being the perfect husband suggested I skipped the match and went shopping for a new dress instead, giving me his card, we made plans for me and Lucy to meet him at the venue at seven instead.

I managed to get a replacement dress. It wasn't as flattering as my original choice but came a close second. A black strapless number. Lucy arrived in her killer heels at six. Some hair curling and a few glasses of wine later we were in the taxi and on our way to the venue. Tim met us at the entrance and looked so handsome in his tux, it was a bit more apparent on closer inspection that he had started the party a little earlier than us.

He was a good drunk, he just became a little louder and a little cheekier this was displayed as he slapped my arse as I walked up the stairs in front of him.

"Now-now, Tim, there will be plenty of time later to mark your territory leave the lovely lady alone."

"Whoops sorry, Lucy did I make you jealous?"

With that he slapped her arse as well, good job I loved him, or I might have taken offence. Instead, we laughed it off and made the way to our table.

Dancing with Lucy, I was enjoying the night Tim was off playing drinking games with his brothers. The room was full, and the auctions had gone well. There was to be one final auction at the end of the night, and then we were off home Lucy was going to crash at ours. Whilst I was attempting to hit the floor in" apple bottom jeans," I felt a tap on my shoulder looking around; I was expecting to see Tim. Instead, I was shocked to see Mathew Mason. I've not see him for thirteen years, and now I have seen him twice in as many months; what are the chances of that. Wobbling on my too high heels, I struggled to keep my balance; a combination of the wine and Mr Mason proximity had me feeling a little light-headed.

"Hello again."

"Hello Amanda good to see you."

He took me by the elbow and led me away from the dance floor, unbeknownst to me Lucy followed.

"Hey Mandy why do you get all the handsome men, don't you think it's time you shared"

She was fluttering her eyelashes at him. If I had attempted the same I would have looked as though I was having a stroke. However, she looked beautiful and sexy and all the things she was attempting to portray.

"Sorry Mr Mason this is my friend Lucy, Lucy this is an old boss of mine Mr Mason."

"Please call me Mathew, Lovely to meet you, Lucy. Amanda excuse me for the interruption I have been watching you and your lovely friend for a while and thought it would be rude of me not to say hello before I left"

Lucy instantly piped up

"You're leaving Mathew why we have only just met, surely you have time for another drink."

Lucy was practically draped across Mathew, and he didn't seem to be objecting. I wish I could say the same. Instead, my chest felt tight, and I had to put my hands behind my back in an attempt not to pull her off him. She has no idea, of course, no idea that this man still owns a piece of my heart and here I am forced to watch, and she turns on her Lucy charm. Needing to get away I edged towards the bar

"I will get the drinks in, whilst I'm at the bar I will see if I can prize my husband away long enough to come over."

Going to the bar, I ordered the drinks plus a double vodka for myself necking it before I made my way back. What followed was one of the most awkward nights I have endured Lucy had her claws in Mathew, and he was lapping it up.

Tim Had decided I was too drunk and he was going to take me home. From what I can make out Lucy and Mathew had decided to go home together, and Lucy had told Tim she would drop me off on the way. Apparently, it would be a shame for me to ruin Tim's night. They don't know the fucking half of it here; I was playing gooseberry between my best friend and the love of my life. I'm sure I have the right to be drunk, I would like to say I got into Mathews car and went back to mine in dignity but the truth is I don't recall. I pretty much can't remember what happened after ten thirty.

M.

Once again, I had been blessed with luck, I knew Amanda, and her husband would be at the venue, but her friend Lucy was an added bonus.

If I played my cards right, she could be the key to my problems. She certainly fit the bill as my potential partner. She would be considered attractive. She was eloquent and well educated. She also seemed interested in what I could offer. Her eyes lingered a little too long on my watch I saw her taking in the cut of my suit and seemed to get a nod of appreciation when she looked at my handmade Italian shoes. Like most women, she weighed me up.

Her charm offensive multiplied once she heard the areas I had property, and what car I was currently driving, her eyes practically rolled back in her head to reveal pound signs when I mentioned my company name. She was mine for the taking should I choose to reel her in. The most delightful part of having her on my side meant I would have access to Amanda.

I was currently driving down a nameless a road on route to Amanda's home with a drunken Amanda sleeping in the back. For years, I have been looking for her, and suddenly fate seemed to be handing her to me on a plate.

"So, Mathew, how do you know the delightful Mandy again? I've not heard her mention you?"

"She worked for me briefly many years ago, how do you know her?"

"We work together have done for a few years, she's a good girl, just has trouble handling her drink."

Looking at Amanda slumped in the back of the car I felt a little saddened that she had sunk so far.

"Does she have a problem do you think Lucy?"

"Well yeah to an extent I would say she does, her and Tim have definitely had words over her drinking I know that much. I thought she may have calmed down a little now they are trying for a baby, but it seems not"

Chucking a look of pity in Amanda's direction Lucy had no idea how important to me that last sentence had been. Amanda was trying for a child; this wasn't something I was happy about. Her body belonged to me there was no way I was allowing her to ruin it by carrying a child. I was attempting a delicate balancing act I needed to proceed slowly and carefully, but once I had my foot in the door, I was going to do whatever had to be done to ensure she never got pregnant.

"If you turn left at this junction we are about ten minutes from their house."

As she said this keeping her voice level, she reached over and put her hand on my knee.

"Once we drop her off what's the plan, Mathew? I would like to go back to yours to get to know you a little better."

I groaned inwardly at her lack of imagination, maybe next she would suggest a coffee. The reality was she wanted to come back for sex, in her mind, it was what I wanted from her. Plastering on my most seductive smile, I turned to look Lucy over.

"Once we drop her off Lucy, I would like to take you back to mine if you want to get to know me more that's fine, but I thought we could leave conversation for a different time, what I have in mind will leave you speechless."

Giving her a wink I was rewarded with her hand moving up my leg to my crotch. Fortunately, I was saved from any further molestation by the sat nav signalling our arrival at Amanda's home, a three-story block of flats hers was at the top.

"I have her keys let me run up ahead and open the door, I hope you're feeling strong, are you okay to carry her up?"

"Yeah fine, run on ahead I will get her out."

Lucy went up the stairs ahead of me, and I opened the back door to retrieve my prize. Leaning over Amanda, I breathed her in. She still had the same old calming smell. Pulling her coat to one side, I was met with her bare shoulder. Slipping her dress down just enough I was rewarded with a pert pink nipple.

Taking my opportunity, I slipped it into my mouth relishing her taste. It felt like heaven after so many years of absence, I was finally home, and I knew one thing for sure, this time she was not getting away. I would have her again regardless of the consequences, I wanted nothing more than to reach between her legs but the cold chill in the air brought me back to my senses.

Cradling her in my arms I carried her up to her bedroom, Lucy stood with the door open a glint of excitement in her eye. To her I must have mirrored her own emotions, my cock was so hard I felt it straining, desperate to be buried inside Amanda.

Reluctantly I put her onto the bed I made my way out, leaving her bedroom door open. Lucy came into my body space reached up and kissed me, pressing her body into mine she gasps when she felt my erection mistaking it for a result of her actions. This was panning out to good. I couldn't have planned it if I had tried. Lucy was feverish with want, so much, so she had no qualms about letting me pull her underwear to one side placing my fingers inside her disgusting wet Centre.

"Shit Mathew I'm not sure I can wait."

Between fevered kisses, I managed to reply me either. Turning her around and bending her over the sofa, I pulled her underwear to one side and entered her. All the while I was able to watch Amanda's sleeping form through the open door.

Lucy like most women was a vocal lover, making a half-hearted attempt be quite, so she never woke Amanda. She squirmed against me. Her actions would normally repulse me, but with Amanda just feet away I was like a fucking stallion nothing was going to sour my mood. Reaching around between Lucy's thighs I brought to orgasm.

Once she was satisfied, I allowed myself to climax, and it was so good. If only we could have Amanda with us every time I would be expected to do this I was sure there would be no performance issues. Once my breathing steadied I politely made my way to Amanda's bathroom to clean myself up.

It was a small room with a basin shower and toilet and a small bathroom cabinet. Opening the cabinet, I saw it was full of the usual bathroom paraphernalia, cleaning products toothbrushes and razors. In the top left corner, I see several pots of folic acid supplements. Many were unopened. So, Amanda was trying for a child. She is such a foolish girl.

This little game of wifey she had been allowed to play was going to have to end soon. She doesn't know yet, but I would rather her dead then have to share her. As we left her flat, Lucy stopped at the top of the stairs,

"Just a minute I almost forgot, Tim, asked that I post her keys back into the letter box before I left"

"Give them here I will do it."

Taking the keys, I made to put them through her letter box instead discreetly putting them into my jacket pocket. Remembering my location, I choose to drive to my London penthouse it was the closest and least personal. The kind of encounter Lucy had in mind was best suited to the sterile environment. Plus, its location would score me further brownie points. Sometimes it amazes me just how fickle some of these women are.

Taking her back to the apartment I kept my promise to make her speechless. Paying her body, the attention she desired. Fortunately, she was exhausted and fulfilled once I had finished with her. I was able to avoid any further penetration. I wasn't sure I could perform as well without Amanda's silent observation.

I woke Sunday morning before Lucy, getting dressed I greeted her with a coffee and my plans for a fictional meeting.

"I wish you could stay, but I have a breakfast meeting, perhaps we can meet up again? If you like?"

Of course, she would like I was her golden ticket.

"Perhaps you should ring Amanda make sure she's well? She was a little worse for wear last night!"

"Yes, I will, I must admit it's getting a little tiresome babysitting her now I really hoped Tim would have talked some sense into her".

Calling Lucy, a taxi I was grateful once she left going to my jacket I took out Amanda's front door keys relishing the feel of the cold steel in my palm. I was back in control, and it felt good before long I would be back in my rightful place as Amanda's Puppeteer.

Chapter 10

Ahh, my head hurts, why do I do this to myself? Looking around my bedroom, I can see no sign of Tim, racking my brains I try to work out how I got home. Taking small, tentative steps, I walk into the living room, Tim's sleeping form is on the sofa.

I decided not to wake him and instead tiptoed to the kitchen. I needed strong coffee before I had to face his wrath. A little ashamed of myself I fought to steady my shaking hands. Sitting drinking my coffee, I tried to piece together the previous night.

I remember dancing with Lucy whilst Tim was at the bar with is brothers, I remember winning an auction for a spa weekend. Gaahh, paying way over the odds. Why am I such an idiot when I'm drunk! I also remember him, Mathew, god that man haunts me I had just got over our last encounter, here he is again infringing on my life with his charm, his smile and his tight firm arse. Worst of all I remember him and Lucy getting on like a house on fire. Why was I so jealous, it's not as though I wanted him for myself?

I'm happily married I'm not about to let a teenage crush ruin that, still I can't help thinking that we had unfinished business. Being jilted by him the way I was we never had a chance to see if we had something special. There was no mention of his wife yesterday, and I don't recall seeing a ring. If this was a mill and boon, perhaps he had sought me out and come back for me. Only to find my sexier taller prettier best friend more appealing instead.

Not sure if I can face this so early in the morning! The impending doom that Tim is bound to lay upon me has me reaching for a little Dutch courage. Hair of the dog being my hangover cure of choice, Vodka of course to leave no trace. In the back of my head I know it's wrong the very fact I have chosen to be deceitful about it means it is, just a little nip won't hurt though just to fight the hangover off for a few more hours.

When Tim wakes up, he doesn't read me the riot act; in fact, it's worse I'm faced with the silent treatment. He is skulking around the flat, cringing away from me if I so much as come within two feet off him. I'm like so toxic chemical if he gets too close his skin will peel. Well, two can play at that game, he is far from innocent if I remember rightly he was half pissed when we got there last night. Okay, so he may not have spent eight hundred quid from our joint savings account on the weekend away, which could have been bought from Groupon for seventy quid. He may not have fallen into a waiter carrying a tray of champagne either.

Grabbing my bag, I decided to get out of his sight. If he found me so repulsive, I would spend the day elsewhere. Checking my bag for my phone as I left I was grateful it still had sixty percent battery. Casting my eyes around the flat, I couldn't see my keys, but I was not going to give Tim the satisfaction of asking if he had seen them. Outside the cold air served well to sober me up. Walking toward the town Centre I reached for my phone, I needed to ring Lucy get this call out of the way it was useless avoiding it. My imagination was probably making things worse than they were.

My imagination could never have been as inventive as Mathew and Lucy were! They had been at it like rabbits according to Lucy, even fucking in my flat. I was grateful that the feelings of jealousy had subsided but in their place, was a burning, overwhelming shame, how after all these years of not seeing him did I have to make such a fool of myself. My feelings of shame aside I found I was quite pleased for Lucy, she was giddy with excitement. She had made plans to meet up again with him in the week, he was smart and sexy just the right side of fifty not to be too old. The sex was amazing apparently, casting my mind back, I can honestly say I don't remember.

It was so long ago, and I was young and inexperienced. I found myself wishing them the best. I was being childish hampering on to my past when I had a bright future ahead of me. All I need to do was make the peace with Tim, and then we could start to work towards it.

Looking at the shop fronts for a peace offering, I settled on the latest console game. Going home my tail between my legs. My return was made harder as I had no idea where my keys were. Knocking at my own front door, I waited for Tim. He answered with a curt nod.

"Where have you been Mandy?"

I was so grateful he had found his tongue, now all I had to do was placate him till peace was resumed.

"Town, I got you this look."

Handing him the game I stood back weighing up his reaction.

"Thank you, but I'm not sure we can afford it now, not with the weekend you bid on yesterday."

I had the grace to look ashamed.

"I'm so sorry about that Tim, I will pay you back, I don't know what come over me I just got caught up in all the commotion" "Mandy there was no commotion it was a silent auction."

Stumped by his reply I could only apologise again.

"I'm just grateful you were too pissed to write anymore number otherwise who knows how much we would be down" "it's for charity Tim."

"Yes, I know that don't excuse it though Man, this isn't the first time you have made me look like an idiot. In front of my brothers as well, first the wedding now again last night they are starting to think you have a problem, to be honest, Mandy you know what, I think, I think you do have a problem. It's not normal to get so drunk you black out. You know, that, right? The thing is I don't understand why you do it, what are you running from? Is our life so bad you need to drink it away?"

Watching Tim his face full of concern I felt so sorry so sad but as much as I promised I wouldn't embarrass him again the one thing I couldn't do was say I wouldn't drink again. I wasn't as bad as he made out a few glasses of wine in the evening was not going to be the death of me

M.

I found a Timpson open and managed to get a copy of Amanda's keys cut. There were three on her key ring, two I assume for the front door the other I didn't know, but I had a copy cut anyway. Jumping back into the car I made my way to Amanda's address.

Knocking at her door, I waited patiently for someone to open it. It took a while but eventually, a dishevelled looking Tim came to the door,

"Hiya, Matt, is it?"

"Mathew, hello, I'm not sure if these are your wives?"

Holding the key up so Tim could see

"I found them in the back of my car this morning, I can only assume they fell out of her bag last night."

He had the grace to look ashamed,

"Thanks, mate, so sorry about last night, thank you for bringing her home."

"That's fine, Lucy was looking out for her."

What I wanted to say was it should have been him bringing her home, what sort of a husband leaves his helpless wife to be carried home by a stranger. He must be some kind of arsehole. It would serve him right should she get into the wrong hands.

"Mathew, do you wanna come in, Mandy's here we were just having a nap I will wake her up she can apologise herself maybe stay for a coffee?"

As much as I wanted to, I didn't want Amanda having a chat with Lucy about me turning up at her door with her keys, as far as Lucy was aware I posted them through the letter box.

"No, it's fine I'm in a rush another time perhaps, Tim maybe don't mention to Amanda I dropped them round there is no need to embarrass her further."

"Okay, no worries mate, how're things go with Lucy? She's a bit of a firecracker that one! Look if anything comes off you two. It will be good to meet up as a foursome? Do me good to have a bloke to talk to them two are a nightmare once they get their heads together".

"Do you know I might take you up on that Tim, Good to see you again, hopefully, see you soon."

Reaching for a handshake, I said my goodbye and left the building? Walking back to the car I resisted the urge to beat my chest triumphantly. Tim wasn't aware, but he was dealing with an alpha male here before he realised it he would be a member of my pack. I felt powerful and strong. For the first time since my heart attack, the dreaded vulnerable feeling was subsiding. I was doing what I do best I was playing God with people's lifes, and I felt good about it. If things went to plan, I would have Amanda and destroy that prick Tim in the process.

I needed to get home I had some research to do. At first, I had ideas about replacing Amanda's folic acid with the contraceptive pill, but it was unreliable, what if she didn't take it one day she could still end up with that moron's baby.

Instead, I would revert to what I knew best I would change them for laxatives. If I was going to invest so much effort in her, I wanted her body to be perfect. Now I needed to find out if the contraceptive injection was something I could buy on the black market. I wasn't one hundred percent sure yet but I seemed to recall it stayed in a women's system for three months before it needed topping up. Ideally, that would be my solution. I had thought about drugging her so I could administer it but it seemed her drinking problem could work in my favour.

Chapter 11

A.

These cold mornings were playing havoc with my sleep pattern, I slept through my alarm this morning. Choosing to stay in my nice warm bed rather than face the cold. Waking with a start I had all of ten minutes to get up washed, dressed and out the door, it was going to be one of them days already. It was only once I got onto the train and was reaching for my phone to pass the time during the journey; I realised I had left it home still charging. Oh, well good old fashion people watching would have to be my morning's entertainment instead. The day proceeded as it had started contractors rang the phone off the hook, supplies sent endless emails chasing payments, and the aircon began soring into life freezing the entire office.

I was glad when home time came around. Once I got home, I checked my phone and see I had a few missed calls from Tim, a text from my sister and a missed call from the Doctors. Ringing the Doctors back I was met with their answer services, seems they closed at six. I would have to ring them in the morning see what the problem was. I waited for Tim to get home and decided to order a takeaway instead of either of us cooking. Fortunately, he was talking to me again, with the day I had I couldn't handle another night of silent treatment.

I got through to the doctors after almost an hour of trying, the receptionist relayed a message, my blood test had come back, and the doctor wanted to see me regarding the results. The next available appointment was two weeks' time. Couldn't be too serious if I to wait that long. The next few weeks went by without incident, once my period had stopped me and Tim threw ourselves back into baby making.

Tim tried to keep things exciting much to my amusement. One evening I came into the flat to find him surrounded by rose petals wearing a PVC thong! I didn't find this arousing, Not in the slightest. Instead, I collapsed on the floor in a fit of giggles. Christ knows where he had bought it from?

"What too much?"

Between bouts of hysteria, I managed to tell him.

"No, it's too little! Tim, you are a gorgeous sexy man, but the sight of your hairy arse hanging out of a PVC thong will haunt me forever! It's like I have stumbled into some hard-core gay sex club!"

He saw the funny side, and we laughed together. I almost wish I had taken a picture to show Lucy. With the weekend approaching, I had made plans to meet up with her. She had been difficult to pin down. She had been seeing a lot of Mathew. At first, it was a little awkward but as time went on it was easier to accept. After a while, I managed to stop thinking of him as My Mathew. The four of us had plans to meet on Sunday for a late lunch. It would be interesting to see how I felt once I see them together but for now, I was happy to separate my Mathew and Lucy's as two different people, after all, it had been thirteen years I had changed so much I'm sure he must of too.

My stomach was a little unsettled this evening, so I choose not to eat before going to meet Lucy. I was hoping my IBS wasn't flaring up. I couldn't help but interpret everything as a possible pregnancy symptom.

We met in a bar and immediately got to work dissecting Lucy's new relationship. She was a beautiful girl, but as with most women she was still insecure, and we spent the evening analysing everything Mathew had said and done. We concluded that, yes, he was a bit older than her but not too old. Lucy was thirty-five, so a seventeen-year age difference was just acceptable. Yes, he was a good catch, and yes, he was very attentive.

We also decided that, no it wasn't a sticking point he had been married before, at his age it would have been weirder if he hadn't. Lucy, of course, pumped me for information once she realised I had seen his ex-wife. I couldn't lie, so I told her honestly that she was probably one of the most gorgeous women I had ever seen.

I tried to settle Lucy's distress by affirming she was easily the second most beautiful woman, but that wasn't good enough apparently. Good job we were good friends as I really wasn't helping.

"It doesn't matter how beautiful his ex is Luce he is with you now, you can't fret about his past, after all, if I'm honest he nowhere near matched up to that Richard you were seeing, wasn't he a dream boy or something?"

"Yeah but he was a complete cock, don't you remember I caught him shagging some bird around the back of the club he was dancing at! Still covered in baby oil the greasy fucker."

"Pa ha-ha, yes I remember didn't he see you make off to run and slipped because the oil was on the sole of his shoes!"

"Ha ha ha yes and the poor girl had no clue what was going on did she? Just stood there with her draws around her ankles."

"There you go then, looks mean nothing. His ex-wife might have been a bitch, whereas you Luce you're a catch! Just a shame about your face."

With that I gave her a wink, she had nothing to worry about she was a stunner. The drinks were flowing, and lack of food meant it went to my head way quicker than I had anticipated, not wanting to have another night I couldn't remember I decided to call it an early night. Lucy never protested she had told Mathew we were meeting for a drink and he had offered to pick us up.

She was more than eager to get back to her booty call. She gave him a quick call, and he appeared within ten minutes. As much as I had put the thoughts of Mathew to the back of my mind my heart still raced at the sight of him, some emotions are so ingrained I guess they are hard to get rid of.

"Evening ladies, you're looking beautiful tonight."

His eyes twinkled as he said it. I'm sure he was talking to Lucy, but as he said it, I couldn't help but notice he was looking at me. Stopping to kiss Lucy on the cheek he asked if he could buy us a drink before we left.

"No, I've had too much, thanks, I should get back home to Tim,"

"How about a quick coffee Amanda help sober you up."

I loved how he called me Amanda, barely anyone did any more; I stopped using it years ago, yet he did, portraying our history whilst doing so,

"That's a good Idea, yes please a small one."

"Lucy do you want a coffee or something stronger?"

She opted to keep the party going with something stronger but Mathew, and I had a coffee, mine tasted a little unusual a tad bitter, but I put that down to this being a bar and not a coffee shop. Finishing up our drinks Mathew and Lucy took me home.

This was, of course, the second time I had been in his car but I couldn't remember the first time. This time I made it home memory intact. A little merry but grateful that I had the willpower to stay sober enough to have an enjoyable evening.

M.

I lie awake unable to settle; I was eager for Sunday evening to arrive. I was extremely conscious of time ticking away.

I had not yet had the opportunity to administer any contraception to Amanda. Fortunately, I had managed to meet up with Amanda and Lucy on Friday evening. I had got some Mifepristone pills from a website. It was an abortion pill that could be used up until the twelfth week of pregnancy. Putting it into her coffee. If Amanda was carrying a little brat that would soon put a stop to it. I enjoyed seeing her and was eager to be alone with her.

At the moment, the negative was far outweighing the positive. I had been spending a lot of time with Lucy laying the groundwork so that we could get some kind of relationship off the ground. I found it so draining. Fortunately, I was able to destress a little by going to Amanda's home and wrapping myself in her bed sheets.

It was difficult at first; I was all too aware that she shared her bed with Tim, but quickly enough I could identify which side she slept on, her body scent hadn't altered, more importantly, the physical reaction the smell evoked hadn't changed. The calm was comforting and serene, Of course, it caused me to become sexually aroused, but I had to squash them feelings down.

I had stooped quite low even by my standards some days I found myself rummaging through her dirty laundry eager to find something only she had touched something that was just Amanda. I settled on a sports bra I hoped she wouldn't miss. I took it with me and put it into my pillow case. It eased my sleep but also at difficult times when I was expected to cement my relationship with Lucy with a physical act I would breathe it in and image Amanda below me.

The first day I entered her flat, about three days after I first started to survey it. I swapped her folic acid for laxatives as I had intended. I felt the power returning. Already my mind felt more at ease my brain a little quieter. With Amanda, back, I could fight the urge to seek out other girls. I could resist the younger ones. Yet I was eager to stop any pregnancy, Sunday needed to hurry up and come around I needed to put further plans into place. Once the possibility of pregnancy was out the way, I could begin to plan how I was going to enjoy her.

Lucy arrived at mine at twelve. We were having dinner at my London apartment, she was eager to cook. Possibly to make herself look more appealing to me, also to impress Amanda and Tim with her cooking skills. I'm sure my apartment lent itself well to the kind of image Lucy was trying to portray. Amanda and Tim were due around three. I fussed around for Lucy putting the champagne on ice for her and helping to lay the table.

I give Lucy credit the food smelt amazing. By the time, they arrived the kitchen was full of the aroma of roast lamb and rosemary. It hadn't crossed my mind that Amanda would be over eating, but now I was acutely aware of the calorie content of the pudding Lucy had painstakingly prepared. It was a small battle to win, but I had intentions of her pudding finding a messy end before it made its way to Amanda's plate.

The champagne was flowing as was the conversation, I was surprised as I found Tim to be quite a likeable character. We shared a mutual appreciation of music, and we had both attended the same university. Although it had been years apart. Perhaps if things had been different, we could have been friends. If he had never met Amanda maybe, but as things were now there was no chance he had taken something which was mine, and I was within my rights to take it back.

Chapter 12

A.

Arriving at Mathews flat, I was impressed with how well he seemed to be doing for himself. I knew he was successful, but all those years ago, when I first started working for him, he operated out of a small run down office; something had changed over the last few years if he could afford this gorgeous rooftop apartment.

It was very masculine, sleek marble surfaces and wooden floors. On our arrival, Lucy led us to the balcony for cocktails The London skyline below was fascinating. I could only imagine how amazing the view was once night fell. The conversation flowed, Tim, joining in referring to how Mathew could stand living in such a slum. Mathew joked along with him mentioning it was just his London home and he had a country shack.

Lucy was eager to show off her culinary skills home baked rolls were served with homemade soup, the main was a roast with amazing melt in the mouth lamb. Between courses we discussed holiday destinations, Tim is well travelled, so he sang the praises of many a far-off island.

"Of course, the most life changing break was my brother's stag do, earlier this year."

"Really whys that?"

"Well we went to France, my brother is a huge Madonna fan, and we went to Paris to see her in concert."

Tim's' cheek flushed at his confession, whilst I'm sure his brother liked Madonna he was more than guilty of singing away.

"let's just say somewhere between material girl and vogue I met Mandy, my fate was set and my own stag do follow six months later, I did email Madge and ask if she wanted to come to the wedding, but nope she never came"

"Six months? So you two had a shotgun wedding."

Picking up my plate to take it to the kitchen I looked at Mathew

"Sometimes when you know, you know."

Rising to help me clear the table he looked at me and replied

"Yes I can relate to that, it's a strange world we live in but every now and then the planets align, and people are thrown together, and nothing and nobody can keep them apart."

Wow, he had it bad for Lucy that was a strong statement from such a normally guarded man, Lucy protested as me, and Mathew cleared the table, but he hushed her and told her to have a break from slaving away whilst we loaded the dishwasher.

It was a poignant moment as we entered the kitchen it was the first time we had been alone together since Scotland, whilst I tried to act normal my body portrayed me as the hairs on my arms stood on end.

Mathew turned and leant against the work surface. His eyes tracing my face.

"Six months Amanda? It's rather quick courtship."

His tone was a little unapprovingly which angered me a little, who was he to judge.

"As I said when you know you know."

Biting my tongue, I fought not to give a testier reply.

"I'm not judging, Amanda don't be so defensive; I'm just saddened, it seems he just pipped me to the post."

Looking at him I struggled to digest his meaning, he looked a little crestfallen perhaps a little sad.

"I'm not sure I get your meaning Mathew?"

"Not to worry, I'm just a silly old man, let's get this dishwasher loaded and back to the table."

As he was saying this he was moving towards me, cocking his head to one side his dark eyes boring into mine, he reached out and tucked a stray lock of hair behind my ear. Such a simple gesture but so personal, so intimate.

My heart quickened, but the overwhelming emotion was the acute awareness of Tim in the other room, my husband, and my love. Perhaps finally the spell Mathew Mason had put on me was broken. For many years, I had dreamt of him coming for me but standing here in his kitchen the spell was broken I saw him for what he was, just a man.

Making our way back to the table Tim was in the middle of a hushed discussion with Lucy, "ooh secrets Tim please tell."

"Nose ointment keep out of it, I'm just asking Lucy's option on a Christmas present I have my eye on for you."

"Christmas it's a little early, isn't it?"

Lucy piped up

"Nope never too early to discuss presents Mand don't discourage him, I think you will love it."

It was a bit peculiar discussing Christmas I had no idea what the protocol was, this would be our first Christmas together. Since Nates untimely death I tend to lock myself away over the Christmas period. Maybe Tim was my chance to wipe the slate clean and make new happy memories. Lucy stood to get the dessert,

"right I hope you all left room as I have made a pavlova with lashing and lashing of fresh cream" "mmm, sound delicious."

Both Tim and I said in unison. Mathew got up to help Lucy, and they both made their way to the kitchen.

"He seems nice Mandy, he really seems to like Lucy! Look at this place she's onto a winner here I reckon",

Remembering the incident in the kitchen I nod, but in the back of my mind I can't help but question his commitment.

My thoughts are disturbed by an almighty crash from the kitchen,

"Everything okay out there."

Tim shouts, rising to my feet I walk to the kitchen to find the floor covered in broken meringue, cream, and strawberries.

"Oh, Lucy what happened?"

"Hmmm, well Mathew was being very helpful, but it seems to have slipped."

Mathew shrugged his shoulders in an apologetic manner,

"Sorry, it looked so nice too."

"It's fine don't worry",

After the Pavlova had made its way to the floor, we decided to crack open another bottle of wine to drown our sorrows. The sun began to set, and we took in the beautiful night view from the balcony. More wine followed, and soon enough I decided that it was best if I slowed down a little. I was eager to make a good impression in front of Tim. On several occasions, Mathew tried to fill my glass becoming a little crestfallen each time I declined. I thought I had done so well, but perhaps the wine finally got the better of me. I remember feeling quite sober and Mathew fixing me a virgin, Mary. But then nothing, the next thing I remember was my Monday morning alarm blaring, waking in my own bed with Tim nowhere to be seen.

Growling as I sat up in bed, I clutched at my head expecting it to be pounding. Fortunately, it wasn't, thank god for small mercies aye, the same couldn't be said for my back side it felt tender and bruise as I bore weight on my left leg. I can only assume I took a tumble. Getting dressed as quickly as I could, I made my way the doctor's surgery for my blood results before I went into work.

The doctor seemed a little concerned apparently, my liver wasn't functioning as well as he would have liked.

"It's something we are going to have to monitor Mrs March, your levels were exceptionally high."

I remained motionless sitting dumbstruck in the surgery

"What causes it, doctor?"

"It could be several things, but it's most likely a result of alcohol abuse."

He looked at me with sympathy

"I like a drink, doctor but I wouldn't go as far as to say I abuse it!"

"you're a small woman Mrs March someone of your build has a lower tolerance than others, in this case, it is generally alcohol or laxative abuse that causes such raised level, I suggest you completely cut alcohol out for six months and then we will do another test."

"Doctor, will it affect my chances of conceiving?"

Moving to the edge of my seat I held my breath and waited for his reply

"To be completely honest I don't know it certainly won't improve your chances, but hopefully you should still conceive naturally."

Leaving the surgery in a daze I made my way back to work, there was no way I could let Tim know what I had done, our chances of a family were slipping away because I couldn't stop drinking, worse of all I was currently getting the silent treatment because of last night. This was something I would have to deal with by myself, one thing was for sure I was ready to stop drinking now. I knew I wanted a child more than I wanted wine.

M.

It wasn't as easy as I would have like injecting Amanda with the contraceptive, she had opted to stop drinking early evening. Fortunately, Tim and Lucy never so they were quite far gone by the time I was forced to spike Amanda's drink. If they thought, it strange that she went from sober to unconscious in a matter of minutes they never let on. I sat and watched as Amanda's eyes began to glaze her speech becoming slightly slurred. Following her into the bathroom, I caught her just before she hit the floor.

Lying her flat on her back I carefully retrieved the syringe from the bathroom cabinet, looking over my shoulder all too aware that Tim and Lucy were in the next room I got to work as quickly as I could. My hands were a little jittery the risk I was taking playing havoc with my nerves. Lifting her skirt, I resented not having time to admire her beautiful form. I stuck the needle into her left leg. It seemed I was becoming a dab hand at injecting her, memories of our Scottish trip flooded back. Smoothing her skirt back down and opening the door I called for Tim,

"Oh, for fuck's sake

Tim fell to his knees and checked Amanda's pulse

"I just found her like this, too much to drink maybe?"

"Yeah looks like it, listen I'm so sorry Matt, again! I think I will take this as our cue to leave."

A cab was called, and they left with Tim giving Amanda a fireman's carry over his shoulder. Lucy was full of apologies,

"I'm so sorry, she is normally such good company, but just lately her drinking is getting a little out of control."

"It's fine, Lucy. It's not your fault, It's Tim I feel sorry for he is clearly embarrassed by her behaviour."

We tidied the kitchen away and chatted for a while,

"Can I stay her tonight Matti, I have my overnight bag."

She looked at me in what she clearly considered sultry licking at her lips. I detested it when she called me Matti, spending this evening with Amanda had left my tolerance for Lucy at an all-time low, I was maintaining this farce so I could get access to Amanda but Lucy was fast becoming a thorn in my side.

"I'm afraid you can't I have an early start tomorrow I have a business trip and need to catch an early plane."

"Oh right you hadn't mentioned it so I just assumed I would be staying over."

Peeling her hands off my chest resisting the urge to snarl

"Well you assumed wrong, I will order you a cab."

She looked upset even going as far as to pout her lips. Turning away from her I rang her a taxi

"Thanks for today Lucy it was nice, you're a very good cook."

She didn't seem to know how to process this looking confused.

"Mathew is everything okay? Why do I feel as though I'm being dismissed?"

Letting out a frustrated breath,

"Come on Lucy don't be so needy it's not becoming, and stop whining, nobody like a whining bitch."

She recoiled at my words

"Your taxi will be her in a few minutes why don't you wait downstairs."

She looked a little shocked but got her coat and made to leave, turning to me she asked

"Will you call me Mathew?"

Knowing I had her hook line and sinker I turned the knife a little more, enjoying her hurt expression,

"Yes, Lucy I will, maybe we should have a small break, though, take a few weeks out, and you could go to the gym burn off some of that excess weight you're carrying? If you lose a few pounds I will treat you, we can go somewhere nice for a weekend?"

The stupid bitch had a million expressions cross her face finally settling on looking grateful as she nodded at me,

"Yes, that would be nice."

Taking her coat, she left.

I slept like a baby, happy in the knowledge that I had achieved what I had set out to do. Waking early my mind had other ideas whilst last night had been peaceful this morning was chaotic. I was eager to get a plan in place so that I might have Amanda again back with me a still silent tiny body beneath mine.

It was going to be far from easy, it seems that I have spent so much of my life formulating plans to have Amanda in my life, I hated her for controlling me the way she did, she was in my every waking thought. For the first time in a long time, I considered if perhaps some of her time was better than none, maybe I should take her as my partner instead of my possession? So many years with her being all consuming had meant the tables had turned. I once considered myself a predator yet here I was time and again brought to my knees by Amanda. Without her calming presence, my life was a chaotic mess she was my anchor the one thing that tied me to humanity. She was so blissfully unaware of how much I needed her.

Maybe with Tim out of the way, I could move in and take his place. Casting my mind back to when we were in Scotland, and I had sex with a conscious alert lively Amanda. I remember it not being as good as before; I remember the thrill not being enough, but now as an older sicker man, I wondered if a consensual Amanda would be enough for me, perhaps it would because the alternative was becoming harder to achieve. It's one thing sedating a young wayward teen to use for my own pleasures, but a thirty-year-old married woman was a harder challenge.

I knew that I would do whatever it took to have her in my life. The need for serenity was spurring me on, each passing day without her calming influence was becoming harder and harder. I was coming apart at the seams. Me, Mathew Chow, successful strong, confident and powerful was being reduced to a jittering wreck because of a stupid woman!

Chapter 13

A.

I don't recall the journey into work, my mind numbed with the news the doctor had given me. The morning went by without me remembering a single call or conversation, I must have been on autopilot. Just before lunch, I pulled myself together to email Lucy, I was aware I needed to apologise and thought I would do it over a nice alcohol-free lunch.

I would tell her I was sorry and I was going to change no more drinking, she was a good friend, and I was aware my actions were driving her away. My email bounced back with an out of office automated response, strange as she hadn't mentioned not being in today. Perhaps she had called in a duvet day.

I would ring her once I get off work. If Lucy wasn't available for lunch I would work through it and leave early, I wasn't fussed about eating my stomach once again in a mess.

Getting home early I decided to make dinner for when Tim got in. I hadn't spoken to him since last night I guessed I was still in his bad books. Whilst the meat was cooking I resisted the urge to reach for the wine, helping myself to tea instead. I grabbed my mobile and decided now was a good time to call Lucy and get the first apology out of the way.

Her telephone rang but she didn't answer, I tried a few times but it rang off each time, I can only assume she was locked up in a love fest with Mathew, that or I had upset her, and she was screening her calls.

Tim arrived home in the foulest of moods,

"Evening, I've made dinner it will be ready for about half an hour."

"I'm not hungry."

"Oh, well it's your favourite I made it especially."

"I said I'm not hungry."

"Tim come on don't be silly, you need to eat."

"For fuck sake, Mandy, what part of not hungry don't you understand?"

It was not often Tim raised his voice I guess I really must have pissed him off! Not content on a night of silent treatment I decided to face things head on,

"Look, Tim, I'm sorry about last night, it won't happen again."

"Sorry? Really, Mandy weren't you sorry the last time at the rugby gala and at the wedding? Eight months Mandy, eight months and almost once a week you're sorry for drinking too much promising you won't do it again!"

Shit that never went to plan I was hoping steak would solve the problem but Tim had really got a bee in his bonnet.

"I am sorry Tim, it won't happen again look I have tea."

Tim grabbed my cup and chucked it at the wall, it smashed and fell to the floor.

"Tim! Please calm down."

I admit I was a little afraid he was normally so loving and caring I suddenly was very aware that although he was my husband, I barely knew him; he was a large man if he chooses to he could hurt me. Cowering back into the corner I mumbled out a further apology.

"Tim please I'm really sorry it won't happen again, please you're scaring me. We are trying for a baby, aren't we? I'm going to stop drinking, and we can have a baby, and it will be great, just like we planned."

He seems to soften, taking my hand in his. His voice took on a softer tone.

"I'm sorry I didn't mean to scare you, but Mandy how can we seriously have a baby you really need to get this situation under control first, it would be irresponsible of me to try to have a child with you. You could be pregnant now, and yet you got completely wasted yesterday with no regard to any unborn baby."

His words stung he was saying he didn't want a child with me!

"But Tim please just one more chance please, it will be different this time, I won't drink anymore. I want your baby Tim, more than you realise. For years, I looked at my sister was kids at a young age, tied down. But it's now I realise, she had a perfect life, she wasn't tied down at all, I want what she has two beautiful babies to love and nurture, I want that Tim I want it with you."

He sighed and shook his head.

"Mandy I can't not right now, look at you the weights dropping off you I would be surprised if you can even conceive your tiny."

I had lost weight recently it was true, but it wasn't drink related.

"I have IBS Tim; I can't control the weight loss, but I can still get pregnant!"

"Don't be ridiculous Mandy look at you, tiny, because you're drinking is more important than food."

I was angry at him I wasn't thinking straight I forgot myself and just poured it all out.

"I can get pregnant Tim, I had done before when I was smaller than this, twice actually, perhaps it's your fucking fault I can't aye? Have you thought of that perhaps too much rugby and being kicked in the bollocks has meant you're less of a fucking man."

As soon as the words left my mouth, I regretted them.

"Oh, my god sorry Tim, I never meant that"

Going towards him he pushed me away, just a tap but it sent me over onto the floor, seeing me on the floor his face took on a look of horror,

"fuck Mandy I need to go, I can't be around you right now I can't be responsible for my actions, I'm going to my mums, look I love you, very much but I can't be torn apart like this by you anymore. I'm sorry, are you okay? Shit I'm sorry, I have to go."

With that he left, he walked out of our flat and walked away from me. Sitting on that kitchen floor a broken mess I needed a drink, instead, I curled into a ball and cried.

It was pitch black by the time the tears stopped. I needed to call Lucy, pour out my feelings she would tell me it was okay and I would feel better, I would give Tim some time to calm down and ring him in the morning. Her phone continued to ring off, so I caught a cab to her flat, she wasn't there, taking a punt I got the cab driver to take me to Mathew's maybe that's where I would find her.

Chapter 14

M.

The intercom buzzed I wasn't expecting anybody, perhaps Lucy had developed a backbone and had come back to tell me what's for, looking at the grainy image on the screen I saw it wasn't Lucy, it was a tiny figure huddled up against the wind and rain.

It was Amanda, she had come back to me. Pressing the entrance button, I let her in, she knocked on the door a few minutes later,

"Hello Mathew sorry to disturb you, I'm looking for Lucy is she here?"

She was dishevelled and sad looking, her eyes glistening to portray her recent tears. She looked beautiful.

"Come in baby girl, what's wrong you look so upset."

She came into the apartment, and I closed the door behind her.

"Is Lucy here, Mathew?"

She looked around as if expecting Lucy to appear,

"No, sorry she's not, I don't expect to hear from her for a while we are on a bit of a break."

She seemed a little surprised by my news.

"Oh, right is it because of me?"

She had no idea how spot on she was, with her here now in front of me and my new resolve to show her the new more honest me I opted for the truth,

"Yes Amanda, it is because of you."

Reaching for her face I followed the recent tear tracks with my finger she pulled away startled,

"Mathew I'm so sorry, please don't blame Lucy for yesterday, it was my fault she wasn't to know I was going to get drunk and ruin the night, I'm so sorry."

With her so sorrowful and ashamed I could barely resist her anymore, so small and broken. Just one more push and I was sure she would shatter before my eyes. Moving towards her I pushed her body against the wall with mine, tilting her head to take her lips with mine. At first, she reciprocated but to my disappointment, she suddenly stopped

"Mathew please I don't understand? We can't do this I'm married."

Pulling her back into an embrace I buried my face into her neck and tasted her beating pulse with my tongue.

"We can Amanda and we will."

Pushing her coat to one side, I sought her tiny breast with my hands. Fortunately, she gave into my advances, I'm not sure I could have stopped myself if she hadn't, I needed her so much, her rejection would have been enough to destroy me. Her tiny small, frail hands were eager pulling at my clothes. I breathed her in committing every sound and movement to memory.

Here I was after all these years, and she was finally back in my arms where she belonged. Between kisses, she made small protests but her body was evidently more eager than her mind. We moved to the bedroom discarding clothes as we went. Falling onto my bed, she finally spoke,

"Mathew, we can't do this I'm married, I love my husband very much."

. I didn't give her a chance to protest any further taking her mouth with mine. The whole time waiting for my disgust to arise. It never came, for the first time in my whole life, I enjoyed the sighs of pleasure. Finding my way between her thighs her sexual arousal was evident and I felt proud to have caused it.

This must be what normal felt like. I curse myself for all the lost years that passed between us. Angry that she could have been with me now and not that wretched man she called her husband. Making love to Amanda that night I felt what every man before must have felt. The physical release was amazing, but the overwhelming feeling was unity. Together as we should be we become one we were one entity. Lying in her arms both of us satisfied I felt more complete than I had ever felt. The moment was spoilt however by Amanda's shudders as she tried to hold back her silent tears.

A.

What have I done! What have we done? I felt awful how could I have done this to Tim, such a kind wonderful, caring man. I had given in so easily, knowing that it would tear my marriage apart. I felt so dirty so soiled.

For years, I had dreamt of Mathews return. Convinced that him wanting me again would make me a better person, a more desirable person. If he comes back to me, it would mean I was worthy. All the doubt that he installed in me would go, all the years of questions about my worth would be answered. I never felt any of these things. There was no overwhelming gratitude as I expected. I must have laid too much responsibility on Mr Mason. For years, his backing was all I wanted.

To have him want me in return would validate me as a woman. I'm not sure when I stopped looking for his approval. No longer aware at which point his rejection stopped controlling my growth, but eventually I stopped looking for him in every crowd, I stopped listening out for his distinctive voice.

For so long he was my every waking thought but one day without realising I found confidence in myself, not needing him to confirm my worth and existence. I stopped imagining I could smell his body on my sheets and feel his eyes on me. He had been a blessing but also a curse for controlling me long after he left me stranded. Sitting here now on the edge of his bed, cheeks still flushed from his fevered kisses, my body recovering from his exquisite assault I realised that Mathew was not good for me.

I needed out of his apartment and fast.

"Mathew, I need to go, I can't stay here, I'm so sorry I should never have allowed this to happen."

Looking around for my underwear the shame was burning at my cheeks.

"Please Amanda sit down, stay with me a while, we have a lot of catching up to do."

"We have no catching up to do Mathew, we only have history, and this should never have happened we should have been content in letting it stay in the past. I'm married and very happy."

"If your happy Amanda, why are you knocking on my door at eleven o clock at night? What kind of husband lets his wife wonder the street alone? What kind of husband leaves his wife drunken and defenceless to be taken home by a virtual stranger? He doesn't deserve you, Amanda."

It took a while to realise that Mathew was referring back to the rugby gala.

"Mathew, Tim is a good husband, it's not the first time I have ruined one of his nights with my inability to hold my alcohol, please don't think badly of him! It's not just about me and Tim either there is Lucy to consider"

Saying her name brought a whole new wave of shame, how could I have done this to her?

"Amanda please just stay a while lie with me a little longer, you have no idea how long I have waited for this moment."

Looking at Mathew he suddenly for the first time appeared needy, He looked as though my refusal would crush him, the damage had already been done what difference would a cuddle make? Lying down beside him, he pulled me in close. I noticed him breathing me in. His hand absentmindedly stroking at my side and hip. It didn't feel right, it was alien this was not Tim. I wasn't nestled against a large bear of a man. Instead, I felt exposed and afraid. What had possessed me to risk so much?

Pulling out of his arms and checking my dress over my head I ran from his apartment grabbing my bag and coat as I left.

M.

I got to her just before she made it out of the door grabbing at her arm to stop her retreat.

"Wait, Amanda, please."

"Ouch Mathew you're hurting me please let go."

I didn't want to let go I didn't care that I was hurting her. In fact, I wanted to hurt her I needed her to be covered in bruises signs and evidence she had spent the night with me, after so long without her I was not about to let her go without a fight. Holding her arm a little tighter I pulled her back closing the front door. Placing my forehead against hers, I tried reasoning with her.

"Stay Amanda, stay here with me, forget Tim, forget Lucy, you're back where you belong now, back in my arms."

"Mathew please you're hurting my arm."

Looking down I realised I was gripping it tightly, releasing it I was happy to see I had left my mark, I was sure that by morning she would have a beautiful bruise to demonstrate my ownership.

"Amanda, please don't run from me, I will hunt you down if you do! You should know this is right we are meant to be together."

Maybe my words were chosen badly as she appeared horrified by my confession, she tried to laugh it off, mistaking my declaration as a joke. Realising I was coming on a little strong, I tried a different tactic.

"Amanda please, I know it's confusing, but for a long time I have been looking for you, for a long time I have needed to immerse myself in you, you don't understand how big a mistake I made letting you get away from me."

"Mathew, it was brief encounter many years ago, surely you are putting too much weight into things, I was a kid when you met me, I don't understand why you are so obsessed you barely knew me."

She was right I was obsessed she never knew the half of it, Of course, it would be weird for me to react this way based on a few reckless nights. She had no idea just how much I had immersed myself in her life. No idea how my heart would beat only for her. How could I demonstrate to her, that she was mine and mine alone without exposing myself for what I was.

"Please Amanda I don't expect you to understand but I think we could really be something special, we could go away together start afresh somewhere just you and me."

I tried to keep the pleading from my voice, tried to hold back some control. She looked at me in despair, and I saw pity in her eyes.

"Don't fucking pity me Amanda" I startled her but the rage was instant

"Please don't shout Mathew you are scaring me."

Still seething from her apparent rejection, I leant in close, forcing her legs apart with my knee, leaning in closer I lowered my voice,

"Don't fucking pity me Amanda if I want you I will have you do you understand?"

She fought back a little this excited me. I didn't see her lift her leg just felt the impact as her knee hit me square in the testicles.

"Mathew I'm sorry about that, believe me, it's not how I envisaged tonight ending, but I am not a thing you can just claim, I am a person, and I will not be dictated to by you."

With that, she turned and left.

A.

I couldn't believe the audacity of the man. What gave him the right to claim me after all this time and demand I leave my husband for him. This had been one hell of a fucking day, in the history of shitty days this one would win hands down. Firstly the news from the doctor then the argument with Tim and now this with Mathew; how did my life go from nought to fucked up in so short a time.

There was only one way I knew how to deal with this, stopping at a late night off license I bought a bottle of vodka. The cab journey home went by in an instant. Arriving back at my flat I never knew what to expect, as much as I wanted Tim to be back, I knew if he sees me coming home at this hour in the state I was in he would put two and two together.

Opening the door, I found I was relieved that he wasn't there.

 Downing half a bottle of neat vodka, I hid the evidence in case Tim came back. I fell into bed hoping sleep would help block out the day's events. As seems to be the story of my life lately the next thing I remember is the alarm waking me up. I was saddened to see Tim had not returned whilst I was sleeping but again a little relieved when I looked down and see I hadn't even showered before falling into bed.

My clothes were a mess, and I reeked of sex. Showering and dressing for the office, I went to work for another day to be spent in a haze. Getting home to an empty flat I decided now was the time to ring Tim; I wanted him home where he belonged, and I needed him back with me. His presence was the only thing that could wipe the slate clean for me. Rid me of the night spent with Mathew. He didn't answer his phone I tried a further six time each time it went to answer services. Not wanting to go to a bar in case I missed his return I turned to the hidden vodka to settle my jagged nerves.

Tomorrow I would stop drinking but first I needed it to blot out the pain I was feeling, the pain I felt because Tim had walked out on me. It was his thought I was drinking, how else was I supposed to deal with his rejection? The more I drank, the more I got angry at Tim's absence. If he didn't want me, I knew someone who did! As soon as the thought entered my head I dismissed it as ridiculous, it was unfair of me to drag Mathew into my marital problems, he was not the answer, If I'm honest he had scared me a little yesterday, so much so I had resorted to violence to get away from him. But the later it got the more I needed someone to turn to. Could he be the answer to my loneliness? Even in my drunken state, I knew the answer. It was a resounding no.

Mathew had been a part of my past Tim was my future. Together we were going to raise a couple of little Tim's and live a long and happy life together. Just as soon as he comes back home.

M.

I paced the floor after Amanda left. Confused at my own response to the evening we had spent together, what had got into me? Why was I suddenly so content to have her on her terms? She had been vocal and fidgety and soft and accommodating all the things that I normally found disgusting in a woman, yet I still wanted her. How had I become so absorbed in her that I was willing to change so dramatically? I didn't need to pretend with Amanda, no longer feeling the need to sedate her to silence her. Yet laying myself bare to her she had rejected me. I'm not used to rejection, very rarely do I set my sights on something and not get it.

I was disheartened at her rejection but not distraught. I knew that her objection meant nothing if I wanted her then I would have her, but unfortunately for Amanda, it would be on my terms.

The week went by without incident, I took the liberty of fitting a few recording devices in Amanda home whilst she was at work, also taking the chance to mix appetite represents in with Amanda's laxatives. I had given her the chance to do things her way, but now it was my way, and she was most likely to suffer as a consequence. It served her right the silly bitch, she had been given the chance to play nicely and had rejected me. That move was going to be detrimental to her. Whilst looking in their medicine cupboard I saw Tim had been prescribed some pain relief, most likely for some sports injury due to rugby, I didn't know what I was going to swap them with yet but knew for certain I would be back with something a little less soothing.

Driving out of London and back to my Suffolk house, my mind wondered to Lucy. She had attempted to call on me on a few occasions, but I had screened her calls; I made a mental note to re-establish contact with her once I was home. I knew one thing for sure, Amanda regretted having sex with me almost as much as I relished it. I would get things back on track with Lucy and make a point of spending as much time with Tim and Amanda as we could. I was looking forward to making her squirm, maybe even arrange a getaway for us all. If I couldn't have her consensually again I was going to get satisfaction from her in others ways, the rejection was becoming a thing of the past instead the future games were exciting me.

Ringing Lucy she, of course, greeted me like a returning hero

"Matti, I'm so pleased you called, I missed you, and how have you been?"

"Good thank you busy with work, how have you been?"

"I'm good, I've been away for a few days. A boot camp you know maybe tone up a little bit."

Smirking at the lengths she would go to in order to please me I chose to throw her a bone,

"I've missed you too Lucy, would you like to meet up soon? I have a trip planned this week but maybe Monday week? We could go for a meal?"

"Yes, please that would be nice, what time and where shall I meet you? "

"I will pick you up from work if you like take it from there?"

Plans were cemented. Putting the phone down, I set to running a hot bath. Sinking into the hot water I began to relax, I felt my muscles unknotting and relaxing. After my bath, I packed my bag for the week; when I told Lucy I had plans I was telling the truth, I had been invited to a private event on Saturday where a few selected girls would be available for gentlemen's pleasure. I had initially declined not wanting to revert to my old ways but with Amanda's rejection still fresh in my mind, I needed to find another nubile body to commit my sins with. Lucy couldn't offer me what Amanda did, the only other source of the elixir I required was found in youth.

Arriving at the agreed location later than I had expected meant that the girls available were limited. I was given a girl who appeared a little ropey around the edges; she was trying to look younger than she was. This was the trouble with some of these events; they were advertised as elite, but in reality, there were many working girls thrown in to make the numbers up. Going into the room I was allocated, I asked the girl to make me a drink; If I couldn't get my thrills from this mutton, I was going to get them elsewhere.

"In my coat, there are some pills; could you get them for me?"

I wasn't a big drug user, but I allowed myself to indulge occasionally. Seeing as my drug of choice currently had me on her rejects list, I was going to use tonight to blot her out of my mind, Popping the pills I went in search of other forms of entertainment whilst waiting for them to kick in. Entering a room, I found two men with a very young girl watching them with her was mesmerising. The fear on her face was almost as intoxicating as the pills that were kicking in. The girl I had been allocated had come with me, she made efforts to engage me whilst I watched the show. I pushed her away as she tried to sit on my lap.

"Sweet cheeks, I'm sorry, but I don't think you can do it for me."

She looked at me slightly puzzled

"I'm sorry, do you mind me saying you don't look the type to be here. You're not the typical clientele."

"Is there a type for this kind of thing? Are you stupid enough to believe a nice man like me fell through this door by accident?"

My words made their way into her thick brain? Startled she asked

"Is there anything I can do for you? "Pointing at the girl in the middle of the room, I reeled off my demands

"Go to her, she looks scared, go to her and whisper into her ear that once those men have finished with her, I'm going to have my turn."

The brass face fell as she realised just how depraved I was. Standing on my feet, she stepped back in shock, she didn't move quick enough the back of my hand contacting her face and knocking her to the floor. Once on the floor, I crawled on top of her lapping away at the blood seeping from a wound on her lip. Pulling her skirt up, I entered her without ceremony the whole time keeping eye contact with the young girl in the middle of the room. I hope Amanda felt proud of herself, she was the only person capable of saving these girls from me; instead, she had driven me to them.

Chapter 15

M.,

Sunday and today is my birthday, myself and the queen don't have much in common, apart from our obvious disdain of public occasions and our love of the races, one thing we do share is I have two birthdays, my real one which is today and my public birthday. It's a long story but let's just say I prefer to spend my birthday away from people. I can't say it's a day of celebration because it isn't, it's more a day of reflection, a day where I indulge and remember what made me the man I am today.

A lot of time and attention is put into this day, I tend to start the planning a week after my previous birthday, I need a week as it tends to take me that long to recover, both emotionally and physically. Generally, the physical recovery is quicker than the emotional one so although it is considered a birthday it's more a birth week. I have hired a house for the event, preferring this as once it's over I am able to separate from it and file it away, never to be revisited until my next birthday. The house was nice, a cosy cottage detached and far away enough from humanity that any screams would go undetected. I took my bags to my recovery room, putting the kettle on there was a knock at the door. My nerves sprang to life I knew what was expected, but I was still petrified of what was to come.

A.

Three days' past and I still never heard from Tim, my emotions were like a rollercoaster ride. The ups and down causing me the mother of all headaches. I swung between blaming myself, blaming Tim and blaming Mathew, what a mess I had made of things, firstly with my stupid behaviour and my inability to control my drinking and secondly committing adultery, should I tell Tim?

I was desperate not to hoping I could pretend it never happened, but what if Mathew told him? It was better coming from me surely. I was so eaten up with emotion it took a while for me to realise I was late for my period; I had installed an app some kind of tracker. Looking at it I see I was a few days late. Perhaps this could be the glue to fix the problems between me and Tim, surely if I was having his baby he would have to come home to me? Angry at myself at the lengths I had sunk to in order to save my marriage, I set out to get a test anyway.

A pee and three minutes later, it was confirmed there is no pregnancy; I'm sad again. It's like every month my body's failure to reproduce is a kick in the teeth, I can't help but assume it's personal, why should I be allowed to have a baby, I don't deserve one! The first hint of temptation and my knickers are in a pile on the floor, Tim deserves someone better someone who can love him and only him!

I'm beginning to feel like I'm drowning in self-pity I don't think I could spend another day in my own company. Life with Tim had shown me what happiness is, it showed me the self-loathing self-pitying women I had been, was someone I did not want to become again, checking my work email I see a message from Lucy, I'm a little apprehensive, afraid what it might say. Fortunately, it's light hearted and humorous; the same old Lucy I know and love, yes, she chastises me for "fucking up her dinner party", but otherwise she seems fine. There is no clue she is any the wiser about Mathew and me, she had some holiday owed and went off to some boot camp apparently.

 Why she needs it, I don't know her body is to die for. Arranging to meet her for lunch, I need to vent so someone, and she is my go to but first I need to get my story straight I need to make sure I exit my infidelity from my tale. Once I have offloaded maybe with Lucy's help, I can work on getting my husband back.

Lucy chose our lunch venue, and it's pretty telling. She chose a local café where the beverage of choice is tea. Maybe it really is time I tackled all my demons. However, the emotional turmoil I was going through at the moment seemed just too daunting, I could only deal with one thing at a time, other people's concerns about my drinking would have to be added to my "to do" list once everything else was sorted I would address it properly.

Seeing Lucy sitting at the table I was flooded with guilt, I was such a bad friend! She looked well though refreshed and polished not a hair out of place, she made me conscious of my own appearance, my dirty blonde wayward hair all over the place. My face looked gaunt a combination of IBS flare up, and lack of appetite meant the weight I gained for my wedding was falling off my clothes hung on what I knew to be a childlike skeletal body. A few pounds' loss to some was quite detrimental to someone of my build.

"Hey baby girl, how are you?"

Reaching and giving Lucy a hug I wasn't even able to mumble a greeting before the sobs started.

"Whoa, Mandy what's wrong?"

Her concerned eyes searched my face, "it's Tim, and he has left me!

"Oh, Mandy I'm so sorry when?"

Between sobs and hiccups, I managed to tell her the whole story. I told her how he blamed my drinking for me not being able to conceive, and I told her how whilst on the defensive I had confessed to Tim that I had done before and it was likely him that was the problem. Of course, I omitted the part where any questions might be raised relating to my unborn child's lineage, the time scale left sketchy.

Lucy was sympathetic and non-judgmental about my abortion; however, she said I was an absolute idiot to challenge Tim's ability to reproduce the way I did.

"There is no way you can blame him, Mand, you have only been trying for a few months, and I think you are both over reacting. He is within his rights to go home to mummy and lick his wounds, you was a bit of a bitch, Mandy, you are gonna have to do some serious arse licking to make up for them comments! But you two will be fine, I've never known a couple to be as in love as you two, he worships the ground you walk on babe, don't threat he will be back soon, you have just wounded his male pride."

I only hoped she was right. "Thank you, Lucy, it's good to get it off my chest" Looking around the café I see my sobbing had drawn quite an audience. Giggling at the old girl's reaction as Lucy stuck her tongue out at her, we left arm in arm to go back to the office.

Getting home that night I felt all the better for telling someone my troubles, chucking my bag onto the arm of the chair I noticed Tim's shoes were beside the sofa, looking around the flat I heard the shower running, pulling together all my courage I went to the bathroom to seek him out. The bathroom was full of steam under the shower stood my husband, I wanted to go to him I wanted to touch him, but I knew I had to make everything good first, he didn't notice me at first as I stood and watched him the pounding of the shower in his ears disguising my arrival. When he saw me he almost jumped out of his skin, I had composed myself to at least try to look sorry but seeing him so startled had me laughing. Fortunately, he wasn't bothered by my apparent lack of remorse instead choosing to cup some water in his hands and chuck it at me instead.

Then stepping from the shower engulfing me in is big arms soaking me in the process, lifting me from the floor with ease and carrying me to the shower dumping me in fully clothed shoes and all.

"Tim, my shoes!"

Laughing at me he pulled them off chucking them over his shoulder. Joining me in our shower, we did all our apologising physically.

Happy Tim was back where he belonged I was content to forget about the last week. Tim being back had wiped the slate clean my infidelity with Mathew a thing of the past, I only hoped it would stay that way. After our makeup sex, we had to face the inevitable and go over our argument. I started with a heartfelt apology,

"I'm so glad your home Tim, I was afraid the things I said may have been too hurtful, I was angry and not thinking straight I was trying to wound you with those words. I'm so sorry I never meant what I said, I know my drinking is a problem, and I will knock it on the head. I want to have your child so much, and it's making me so anxious. I know it's not the answer but drinking is how I deal with anxiety."

Give Tim his due he sat and listened to me without interruption.

"Mandy, I understand you come from a drinking culture, you turn to it for many reasons stress, celebration, because it's a Wednesday. But you need to understand that it's got to the stage now where it is changing you as a person, the second you stop being able to function on a human level and pass out surely that's the point you need to think it's not good for you.?"

I nodded in agreement, I wanted to argue that's it's not every time and there are times I can function perfectly normally, but I knew today was about grovelling not arguing.

"Mandy, you were very hurtful; I know you were trying to be hurtful, so I never let your comments bother me. I'm twenty-eight fit and healthy, I don't doubt for one second I am fertile, these things take time, even a dumb arse like me knows that for the record I'm pretty attached to my bollocks; as a result, I keep them quite protected during rugby matches. My head is a different story, but my balls have suffered minimal damage."

His smile melted my heart, such a beautiful smile such a caring man, snuggling up into him I enjoyed having him back next to me back home where he belonged.

"There are a few other things we need to talk about Mandy, not now if you don't want to but one thing we need to really address sooner rather than later, your weight loss, I've been gone less than a week, and you are shrinking before my eyes. It's not as though you were carrying much weight anyway but now you are positively tiny, I think you should book a Doctor's appointment, see if you can treat this IBS properly?"

At the mention of the doctor's, I was suddenly reminded of the last time I was there when they told me about my failing liver functions. Trying hard not to portray how anxious it made me I agreed to book the next available appointment.

Chapter 16

M.

Opening the door, I was met with my appointment, I had seen photos of who was coming, but I was still startled at how well they fit the brief. The man was tall, maybe six foot, around my age with silver hair and startling blue eyes, his presence stirred something inside me; I recognised it as fear. The female a tiny woman in height and weight, her hair shorter and lighter but still holding the same dirty blonde tinge needed to bare resemblance. It wasn't as difficult as people would expect; finding someone who was in such advanced stages of anorexia, there are a lot of sites that celebrate how thin they could become. What was difficult was getting someone to agree to my plans. Once I had picked her from the site money done most of the talking. It seems everyone has a price.

They both entered the house I offered them a drink and gave them a chance to get settled in their rooms. Going to my own room, I sat on the edge of my bed dangling my feet sucking my thumb. I sat for maybe half an hour before the man appeared. His approaching footsteps had my heart racing in my chest. Apprehension and fear left my breath coming in short, sharp gasps. I knew what was coming and still, I was petrified

"Matti, what are you doing? Stop sucking your thumb, you stupid boy."

His words sent a chill down my spine

"Sorry father, I'm so sorry."

My own voice felt small and weak

"Come here your sister is ready for you."

"Father no please I don't want to."

Smack, a fist connected with my face, a powerful blow which had me seeing stars, the man looked at me at first concerned he had been too rough, looking back at him I snarled

"Keep to script."

A curt nod, the man grabbed me by my ear and tried moving me from my bed,

"Father please no, not tonight, it's my birthday I don't want to."

"Matti it's because it's your birthday that you have too!"

Another blow this time to my stomach saw me collapse to my knees. I was recovering from the blow trying to catch my breath when another blow this time from his knee connected with my face,

"Come, Matti, it will be fun, now let's not leave your sister waiting."

I followed him, of course, I always did. We found the women in the room I had set aside for us. She was so frail so beautiful. Looking her over she had the same gaunt look to her face, months maybe weeks from death she carried herself the same as my sister. Hunched overhead down almost like the strain of moving her frail body was too taxing. She looked at the man and began her script, she was word perfect almost as though she wasn't acting at all.

"Please daddy, not tonight, I'm unwell I can't."

"Heather, what happens if you protest?"

I cowered in the corner, I knew what happened. A punch to my ribs had me double in pain, Heather screamed

"Daddy no, please leave Matti alone it is his birthday, Daddy please,"

the man playing my father was doing a good job, so good that I stopped seeing him instead filling in the events from memory, my father laughing hysterically, all the while kicking at me on the floor,

"Happy birthday Mathew, what are you ten, eleven? Eleven, that's right stand up boy, stand tall."

More hysterical laughter followed.

"That's right you can't stand tall can you, you're a tiny little mouse!"

Eleven punches I had to endure, he made me count. When he got to five, I blacked out. Water thrown onto my face brought me round for the remaining six. My eyes were swollen my mouth full of blood.

"Now for the celebration Matti, come here my boy."

Moving toward Heather I couldn't look her in the face; instead I looked at the floor, "look at your sister Matti, look at how pathetic she looks, so fucking skinny, Heather show Matti how skinny you have become let him see you, Matti look up!"

I didn't want to, but I had no choice my father pulled my head up by my hair.

"Come, Heather, he is waiting, show your brother."

with that my sister began to peel her clothes away, I didn't want to look I didn't want to find her arousing but as she removed her clothes and dropped them to the floor my addled confused eleven your old body reacted, the same way it always did when daddy wanted us to play nicely together

"Look at her Matti, look how skinny and scrawny she is now, she did it to herself you know! So I wouldn't want her anymore, it worked she disgusts me! But you like her don't you Matti."

My father grabbed at my prepubescent penis which to my shame was erect, a result of my own sister's naked body before me.

"look, Heather, your brother will have you even if I won't, open your legs Heather let him see you properly."

"No daddy please!"

Another blow hit down upon me this time to my ribs causing me to cough and splutter. Heather did as my father asked not wanting him to hurt me anymore.

"Look, Matti, your sister has a present for you."

Coming back to the present I found I was lying on the woman the feel of her so slight below me. The man looming above us as he held my head back by my hair, the pain was immense it took all my willpower not to fight back. He knew what he had to do, and I knew what was coming, but the shame still hit me, much stronger than any of the punches and kicks had done.

Taking my erect penis in his hand, he guided it into the women. I was inside her for a minimal time when the orgasm seeped out of me. There was no euphoric pleasure no release just shame and sadness. The man left but not before pulling me off the women and pounding blow after blow into my abdomen and chest, once he left I went back to her I lay cradled between her thighs. By mind numb, as she stroked my hair and comforted me. This is when the peace comes. Lying there with this woman who was playing the part of my sister, both of us having been through an unspeakable ordeal. Victims together in my father's sickening games; I hated what my father did to us both, but those moments when he left us alone, and she cradled me and loved me, I was almost grateful to be there; I was grateful because I got to have her hold me and I got to feel her frail still failing body beneath mine.

I must have slept, that or lost consciousness, I was aware of coming back to reality, and the woman had gone, the blood on my face had dried. Looking down at my battered body bruises were beginning to appear. Making my way to my recovery room, I showered and put on some clean clothes. Going downstairs was a laborious task. Stopping every few steps to rest. I could hear the noise of murmuring voices, they were in the kitchen seemingly enjoying a bottle of wine. The man looked up and spoke first

"There you are mate, I was getting a little worried about you."

The concern in his eyes confirmed this to be true

"No need to worry I'm fine thanks!"

"You sure? That's a nasty cut you have to your lip do you want me to look at it for you?"

Putting my hand to my lip, I felt the welt of a cut

"No, it's fine thanks, I have a nurse coming in tomorrow, thank you anyway."

"You sure mate I was a paramedic once, a lifetime ago, I can just dress it with some butterfly stitches, minimalize any scarring?"

It was an appealing prospect

"Okay if you don't mind?"

"Not at all, come here."

With that, I made my way over to the kitchen stool, and this giant of a man tended to the wounds he had caused. He had changed out of the shirt I had requested he wore and was wearing a cable knit jumper; as a result, he looked a little less threatening. However this close to him, I could still make out a hint of my father's aftershave.

Attention to detail had been paramount for the role play. He was good on his word cleaning the cut and putting butterfly stitches on my face to stem the bleeding, the women was a little less vocal, she just sat back looking at us with inquisitive eyes. Finally, she found the courage to speak.

"Was that okay for you, Mr Black?"

She used an alias I never used my own name during these encounters not wanting to be tracked down by my employees after an encounter.

"Fantastic poppy, thank you very much, I hope it was okay for you?"

"yes, it was, I was a bit worried as it's the first time I have done anything like this for money and well the violence was a concern I admit, but it wasn't as bad as I imagined, still very concerning though Mr Black, are you okay? You got quite hurt in there?"

She looked at me with sympathy, I knew her real concern was not for the grown version of me but instead of the boy that had been through the trauma in the first place.

"Thanks for your concern poppy, I'm fine, now would you and Mr Greggs like to join me in something to eat before you get back?"

Maybe I shouldn't have been so cruel, I knew she would refuse and expected her to be a little ashamed at having to do so, but she was a strong woman, stronger than her body implied that was for sure. She had chosen to be the way she was, and by minimalizing her food intake, she had done as many before she had. She had taken back control.

"No, thank you, Mr Black, as you can see, I have a figure to maintain; you don't get hip bones like this without putting in some hard graft."

Winking at me I could only laugh at her comeback.

"Fine then shall we have more wine instead?"

I was met with two yeses, I had to point Mr Greggs in the direction of the wine as I was starting to feel the consequences of our evening. I was pretty sure I had a few broken ribs, and my eye had swollen at an alarming rate. I was sure I looked like the elephant man. Poppy left after the second bottle, I called her a cab and paid her the remaining balance of her agreed fee. Mr Greggs stayed a little longer waiting for Poppy to go before he started to fuss about my physical condition,

"I've done a bit of a number on you I'm afraid mate, will you let me put some witch hazel on your bruises?"

I enjoyed the attention he gave me cleaning the dried blood that had gathered around my cuts. Helping to remove my shirt he confirmed what I already knew, it seemed I had two broken ribs.

"He really fucked you up there your old man aye?"

I was taken back by how blunt he was, I was used to getting sympathy from the women, but generally, the men left with their fee as soon as they could,

"You could say that Mr Greggs."

I wasn't sure I wanted a heart to heart right here in this kitchen with this man, so I kept my answers short.

"Was everything okay, though, was it how you wanted it?"

"Yes, it was fine thanks."

Grateful for the time and attention he was lavishing on me I decided to engage him in conversation after all.

"I hope it wasn't too distressing for you Mr Greggs, I know it's quite a horrific role play that's why I pay so well."

"It was fine, you will be surprised what I get asked to do being in this line of work, mostly it's me getting a whack, so it was a good job, just ...well"

Looking at him I wasn't sure what he was going to say

"Well spit it out what's the problem?"

I was expecting him to ask for more money.

"How can I put this? I do this line of work, mostly for the money it pays bloody well but also for the kicks, I never got any today Mr Black, I'm going to have to go home rather unfulfilled."

Laughing as I got his meaning,

"Sorry I didn't think, I'm sorry as you know Poppy's gone which is a shame as I'm sure she would have accommodated you."

He looked me up and down and what he said next took me completely by surprise, I was hoping you could deal with my issues, to be honest mate."

I almost spat my wine out I was so surprised, more so by just how blasé he was being about it.

"I'm not sure it's my scene, to be honest with you, you're a tad too old for my liking not to mention manly!"

This was by no means part of the script it was the first time I had ever been approached sexually by a man, and if I'm honest, the idea didn't totally disgust me.

"It's up to you, but you can't blame a man for trying!"

By the third bottle of wine the pain was at a minimum, we had moved on to whisky and moved from the kitchen into the more comfortable lounge. The conversation flowed, and I was happy to let him stay, I needed him to help me to bed as at this point whilst the pains had numbed my body was failing me. Normally I would have made my way straight to the recovery room, and the nurse would have come to me in the morning. Today's evening had panned out a little different to how it was planned. The clock struck twelve signalling the start of a new day

"It's no longer my birthday, today I'm free again."

If he knew what I meant he made no sign of acknowledgement.

"I think it's my bed time now Mr Greggs, could you help me please?"

He took me to my room where I paid him the other half of his fee, and he left. Lying in bed waiting for sleep to claim me I did wonder to myself what if, what if I had explored that side of me allowing myself to take him up on his offer, how would it have been? Would I still have craved the same thing in a man that I deemed necessary in a woman? What kind of dynamics would there have been between us? All these thoughts were running through my head when I realised the enormity of what had gone on today had barely registered.

When it did hit me it hit hard, I'm no Freud, but I know why I am the way I am, but knowing doesn't make the part where I was made this way any less painful.

I will not cry, crying is for weak people, but I was overcome with such sorrow for that little boy, such sadness for what he had become. Sleep finally beckoned me, and I woke hours later when my nurse let herself in.

"Hello Mathew let see what we have here then shall we?"

She pulled back the sheets,

"Ooh, you took a beating boy a good one at that, what's on your face though someone has tended your wounds."

"Morning Mavel, yes one of the people I had over were ex-paramedic they cleaned me up, how have you been? It's been too long!"

Mavel had done this job for me longer than I could remember, my Aunt from my father's side. She would tend to me after these occasions. Whilst most people were on my payroll Mavel would send me out of the goodness of her heart, she was also one of the only women I felt deserved my trust. She was getting on now maybe approaching seventy-five.

Changing the butterfly stitches and giving me pain killers she helped me dress and we went down to the kitchen, she had cooked a full English, I enjoyed spending time with her she was probably one of the closest things to a mother I ever had. Yet our relationship was far from conventional

"How have you been Mathew is life treating you well?"

"Yes, thank you, as well as can be expected, how are things with you? How are things at home?"

"not great Matthew, your father, is ill, he is getting worse as the weeks go by, you should come to see him Mathew make your peace with him before it's too late,"

"Mavel you know I can't do that."

"Please Mathew he is no threat to you anymore he is an old man he can't hurt you!"

Her voice held a note of pleading.

"I'm sorry but it's a no, I can't, I'm sorry, I can't forget Mavel; it's not so easy."

"I don't expect you will forget whilst you insist on reliving it every year Mathew, look at you almost broken, paying someone every year to remind you that you should hate your father, your just like him you know just as stubborn."

I wanted to disagree I wanted to say I'm not like him that I was a different man a better man, but I knew it to be a lie.

For five days, she came in and tended to me, making me an evening meal as we sat and chatted about trivial things, my body was recovering quickly by the third day the cut on my lip had closed. By the fifth day, I was recovered enough that I didn't need her to come anymore, we said an emotional goodbye until next year. I went back to London a few days earlier than anticipated and went back to what I do best, watching Amanda.

Chapter 17

A.

Christmas was fast approaching, I hated the hustle and bustle of Christmas shoppers; so, I and Tim hit the shops early. I had to buy for my nieces and sister as well as Lucy, Tim had to buy for his parents, brothers, nephews and sister in laws. As an early present to each other we decide to take the weekend break I had bid on in the auction, so we find ourselves doing our Christmas shopping in Madrid.

The high street was a mix of designer clothes shops with quaint Spanish restaurants thrown in, it was a cosmopolitan city with beautiful old building mixed with new sleek ones. Sitting in a corner café eating Parma ham and olives we sat enjoying the parade of people walking by, the bull ring was to our left a huge structure with statues of matadors and bulls in bronze at its front. It seemed peculiar that such a barbaric ancient sport was still thriving in such a modern city. The old mixed with the new. I was lost in thought when Tim interrupted with his itinerary,

"I have two presents left to get Mandy then I think we should visit the plaza, what do you say?"

"hmm hmm, sounds like a plan."

Deep down I was done with shopping and site seeing I wanted nothing more than to find a nice bar. Tim to his credit had chosen not to drink around me as a sign of solidarity for me remaining sober. He was coping quite well, much better than I was. There had been a few lapses which I think I got away with. A few occasions when I had a few vodkas miniatures, just to steady my nerves or calm myself after a stressful day. I was confident I would be able to have a few vodka miniatures before we took off on our sightseeing tour I just needed to make my excuses get to a shop as I had exhausted the mini bar. Time was ticking by, and I was getting more desperate I decided to chance my hand and suggested a glass of wine to go with our food,

"Just the one, it's a shame not to Tim don't you think?"

He seemed to think about it for an age finally agreeing,

"Okay, just the one?"

When the waiter came, I ordered a bottle, at least this way I would get two glasses. The food was pleasant the wine was flowing, and I found myself relaxing in my own skin. I was happy to take to sightseeing with gusto once the wine had done its job and relaxed me. Feeling happy and content we explored Madrid. Stopping to take yet more photos Tim insisted I pose in front of a statue.

"Don't you have enough photos of me, Tim?"

"Just making memories Mandy" pulling me in for a couple's selfie.

"Where let me see, oh god Tim delete that one, I look awful, my eyes are shut."

He did as I asked. Looking through the camera reel, I noticed how thin I was looking. Next, to Tim, I looked like a child.

Exhausted from shopping and sightseeing we made our way back to the hotel. My feet were throbbing. We lay on the bed whilst Tim searched through the TV channels for something to watch. I took this opportunity to take a bath and soak my aching feet, I had visited Ann summers before we flew out so wanted to surprise Tim with my new purchases. Once I was clean and dry I struggled into an outfit which had cost a fortune, putting on my highest heels I looked myself over in the mirror, not too shabby hopefully Tim agreed.

Opening the bathroom door and building courage to go outside. I walked out with a

"ta-da"

I'm not sure why, to be honest, not much sexy about a "ta-da "but I wasn't sure what else to say. I was greeted with a long-drawn-out snore, Tim was sounding on the bed. Not impressed with my husband I decided to go back to the bathroom and put on my comfy PJs, but not before I took some photos of myself on Tim's phone so at a later date he could see what he missed out on. Tim is such a heavy sleeper I couldn't have woke him if I tried. Posing beside him in my most provocative manner I was giggling away to myself as I snapped away.

The flight home Sunday was uneventful, I wish the same could be said for our return home. Getting to the front door, I knew something was wrong; the door was ajar, Tim went in in front of me checking the coast was clear. We were met with total carnage the whole flat was upside down, draws emptied, clothes were thrown all around the room the TV was on the floor, Laptops smashed. I would say it looked like we had been robbed but we clearly hadn't, everything of value had been destroyed but not stolen. Checking the door, it seemed undamaged.

"Mandy, you were the last one out the door, are you sure you locked up?"

"God, I don't remember Tim, I would think so but it's not unheard of me to forget to close the door is it! I'm so sorry I was so excited to get to the airport, I really can't remember".

We rang the police who assumed that it must have just been kids, seeing the door open they probably took a chance and went in. They dusted for prints all the same. I was gutted, there had been a few occasions when I had returned from a day's work to find the door open, it wasn't unheard of for me to race out and not close the door properly. We made a start on tidying up, but it was a long process.

The mindless damage was so distressing I found broken glass in the shower, even the clock on the kitchen wall had been smashed down. Fortunately, we had contents insurance but replacing it was going to be time-consuming and stressful.

"We should be grateful that they never took anything really."

"I don't agree with you Tim, if they had taken stuff at least it would have justified it, this, well this is just bastard kids look what they have done! Destroyed someone's home, and what for, fucking fun!"

"I know baby, but they were opportunist if we had been robbed you would have been worried about them coming back wouldn't you, would have felt more violated, we would have needed to change the locks."

"I think we should still change the locks, just to be sure! The insurance covers it after a break in so we should get them done."

"Yeah, fine whatever will make you feel safer,"

I had to book the next few days off. Fortunately, the bosses were understanding. I waited in for the locks smith and had a major tidy up. The cheque from the insurance company took its time but we borrowed money from Tim's parents to replace everything, we were lucky and managed to get everything in one shop, and they delivered. Tim couldn't get the time off, but he still spent the next few evenings setting up TVs and laptops so that we were back to square one.

Feeling thoroughly deflated I went to the kitchen to dish up a takeaway. Tim finally got the chance to upload the Madrid pictures. I had forgotten about the underwear pictures I had taken in the hotel until Tim nuzzled into my neck, his erection pressing into my back,

"What are these? You cheeky little minx!"

"Ha ha ha, I had forgotten about them."

Turning into his embrace

"Do you like?"

"Do I like? Hmm, I fucking love!"

Lifting me with one arm onto the work surface, he started to unbutton my shirt, leaving a trail of kisses down my neck to my breast.

"First, wifey I must have you, now! Then you are going to put this on, and I'm going to fuck you again, is that clear?"

Squirming against him I shifted so he could remove my jeans.

"I like when you're dominant Tim, tell me what are you going to do to me?"

He did tell me, then he backed it all up with the most amazing sex. How did I get so lucky? Such a fantastic man who fulfilled me in every way. I was gutted we had been broken into, but life was too good I wasn't going to let it bring me down.

Chapter 18

M.

I was looking forward to seeing Amanda, the Friday evening I positioned myself outside her flat and waited for her to return home. By ten it was apparent, she was not going to. Conscious that if I went into the flat, she could return any minutes I instead had to wait in the car. If she had been out for the night she could return anytime between now and early hours in the morning, I was cold tired and grumpy, but I couldn't leave now as I wouldn't know where she was.

The clock ticked by slowly I was getting colder and colder but couldn't put the engine on as it would draw attention to me being there. By four I had no choice but to go back home, driving home I was so angry speeding down the A13 I got flashed by a speed camera. Checking my speedometer, I was doing a hundred and three. Banging the steering wheel in frustration, another misdemeanour I could chalk up to Amanda. She was beginning to frustrate me, there seemed to be so many negatives connected to her right now. I was behaving erratically which made me even more frustrated.

I went back to her flat early Saturday after very little sleep. I had no choice but to knock at the door, If Amanda opened the door it would serve her right should she panic and assume I was there to spill the beans about us. If Tim answered, I would make up some lame excuse about looking for Lucy. I knocked and waited, knocking again I took a chance and opened their door with my key. I was taking a risk it was the first time I had been in at the weekend, as a rule, I go during the week when I know they are both at work. Opening the door, I listened for any movement, there seemed none. Sweeping the flat to confirm it was empty I locked the door from the inside should they return I would be alerted to it, not that there was any exit other than the front door, but at least I would get a heads up.

Lying on Amanda's side of the bed I breathed her in enjoying the relaxing feeling that swept over me. Where could they be? Searching through their bedroom nothing seemed out of place, on the floor in the bedroom I found an empty bag, inside was a receipt for underwear, stockings, crotchless panties and a bra. I instantly saw red. She was dressing like a slut for that fucking man before I realised what I was doing I had cleared the content of their dressing table with one fail swoop. Her perfume smashed onto the floor along with a jewellery box and Tim's aftershave.

Moving into the living room I smashed everything I could see, the TV, the computers, the mirror, I wanted to hurt her, the way I was hurting, I wanted to hurt Tim, who did he think he was taking what was mine! What had been mine for the last thirteen years? She had been made in my sister's image for fuck sake! The chances are she was mine when she was fucking born, how dare she shut me out. I had told her how I feel, I had offered myself to her and she still chose him! The penniless retard. Didn't she know what I could do for her all that I had could be hers! I needed her more than I had ever needed anyone and she didn't care, she could not care less she was so fucking self-centered.

Eventually, the red mist cleared. My breathing regulated and I uncurled my clenched fists, the tightness in my chest remained. Deceit and hurt burning away at my already damaged heart. Looking around their flat, I was ashamed I had lost control so easily. Clearing a space on their sofa, I sat and surveyed the destruction. I didn't feel guilty. It served her right for dressing like a slut and whoring herself out. I felt lighter for getting some revenge. I needed more, I wasn't sure how but I was going to cause them both more distress.

Before I left, I checked Amanda's appetite suppressants, and laxatives were fully stocked. Looking through the cupboards I was hoping to find some more medication that belonged to Tim, not sure what I would have replaced it with if I had found anything. His rugby ailment seemingly better I found nothing. Stepping across the broken glass, I made my way out of their flat. Monday, I would reconnect with Lucy, it was clear I needed her so I could get the inside scoop. I was also set on finding a way to hurt Tim I was no longer prepared to let his actions go unpunished.

Chapter 19

A.

After the break in things had seemed to run along smoothly for a while, I was aware that Lucy had hooked back up with Mathew, but so far, I had been able to avoid meeting up with them. Tim had seemed quite fond of him, and on several occasions, he suggested meeting up with them for a drink or dinner, but I always managed to deter him, I was afraid what the outcome would be should we meet up.

Mathew had made it clear that he wanted to pursue a relationship despite the fact we had only spent one night together, I can only assume I reminded him of his past, perhaps reminded him of a younger version of himself. I didn't see that I could offer him anything that Lucy couldn't and the fact their relationship seemed to be going strong gave me confidence that our night together had been forgotten about.

It was a week before Christmas, historically this is a difficult time for me; the memory of Nates accident is always so clear and so vivid at this time of year. This year was to be different however I had a wonderful husband who I intended to make new Christmas memories with, we had been out and bought a real tree. It was the first time I had bought one, normally mum would settle for dragging out the same old artificial one every year. I loved the smell of the real tree, every time I opened the door to the flat I was met with a beautiful Christmassy aroma. It was saddening to think we couldn't keep it after the twelfth day. I had thrown myself fully into Christmas this year, and after weeks of feeding my Christmas cake, I was now icing it in preparation for Christmas day. It was getting late Tim should have been home an hour ago, I assumed he had gone out on a last-minute Christmas piss up, there was some left-over brandy from feeding the cake and before I realised I had finished the bottle, Christmas carols playing on the radio.

The brandy working its way through my body I felt warm and festive. The house phone rang, breaking through my concentration, abandoning the iced tree I was attempting to construct, I skipped over to the phone whilst singing to a Cliff Richard song. The landline phone never rang unless it was a cold caller, picking up the phone I waited for the tell-tale silence to indicate a call from abroad. Instead, a female voice spoke clearly down the line.

"Hello, could I speak to Mrs March please."

"Hello, yes speaking "Mrs March My name is Beatrice I'm calling from Queens Hospital, I'm afraid your husband has been involved in an accident."

I couldn't tell you what was said next the shock truly kicked in, it was like history repeating itself. Putting the phone down I tried to ring Lucy, my hands no longer belonged to me they were shaking so much it took two attempts to hit the right buttons on my mobile. I needed to get to the hospital fast, Panic set in as I waited for Lucy to arrive my entire body shaking with the shock. My mind shocked into numbness, I can only assume it shut down as a self-defence mechanism, but I was so cold. It could have been two minutes or two hours when the doorbell alerted me to Lucy's presence, falling through the door into her arms I saw she had Mathew with her.

"Mandy, what's happened?"

"I don't know Lucy I only know he is hurt and I need to get to the hospital, can you take me please?"

"Of course, we can come on grab your coat, it's cold out, we will get you there as quickly as we can".

I didn't scream or cry in Mathews car not as I would have expected instead I sat numbed and silent, why do bad things keep happening to me! Why again, please let him be okay I love him so much! Getting to the hospital Lucy took over, I was a jittering wreck by this point. We were directed to ICU. Finding Tim sitting up in bed and conscious I almost fell to the floor as relief flooded over me, Mathew caught me just as my legs began to buckle. With a weak voice, Tim spoke,

"Mandy darling you look a lot worse than I feel."

Even in a hospital bed he was more worried about me, I fell onto the bed sobbing into his lap

"What happened, Tim? I thought you were dead, why are you here?"

"Maybe that explains why you smell like a brewery then babe aye!"

Despite the circumstances, he still managed to look at me with disapproval, I found myself trying to make excuses,

"I was feeding the Christmas cake when the phone rang I must have spilt brandy onto myself".

He looked at me with total disbelief. I changed the subject quickly

"Enough about me baby, what happened"

Confusion crossed his face

"I'm not sure; to be honest, I went out at lunch for some sandwiches. I can't be certain but from what I can work out a kid ran at me, they had a hoody on, I thought they punched me in the side. I was winded but confused more than anything; it wasn't till I got into the sandwich shop I realised I was bleeding; the bastard had stabbed me mand!"

His voice caught in his throat; it was like telling me the story had made him realise the gravity of the situation. He looked at Lucy and Mathew embarrassed as tears threaten to fall. Lucy took the hint

"Mathew and I will go for coffee, give you two some time together, do you want anything?"

"no, thank you."

with that, they left, and Tim's flood gates opened, I have never seen him cry and seeing him so weak, so confused as to why this has happened to him I sobbed along with him.

Tim had been lucky an off-duty surgeon had been getting their lunch at the same time so could stem the bleeding whilst they waited for an ambulance. The knife had missed any major organs. With a few weeks' bed rest, he should make a full physical recovery, I wish the same could be said for his confidence. He had been reduced to a nervous wreck even walking around the hospital ground had him behaving like a rabbit in the headlamps. Everybody was treated with suspicion a possible threat. My poor big strong man was afraid of his own shadow. It was made worse as there didn't seem to be any motive for the attack it seemed to be totally random.

Our return home was fraught with security check after security check, paranoia had Tim convinced the knife attack, and the break-in was related. Whilst I didn't think they where I found it was easier to agree with him, to challenge him would result in him losing his temper, shouting and hollering at me like he had never done before. Whilst he seemed to suddenly be afraid of potentially everyone. I became his verbal punch bag. What is it they say? It's often those we love that we hurt the most.

Christmas was a quiet affair in the end. A few days after Tim was released we travelled to his parents' house, they lived in a quiet village where everybody knew each other it was less likely that Tim would feel vulnerable. Instead of Christmas carols at midnight and Boxing Day spent in the pub, we settled in for eggnog around the log fire. It was still pleasant probably more so than if we had stayed at home. But my husband had lost his sparkle. I was aware that I would need to help him get over his ordeal; he needed me now more than he ever had, I only hope I was up to the job.

Chapter 20

M.

I hadn't intended to hurt Tim in the literal sense, but I had become desperate. After I had trashed their flat, I had gone back a few days later to find the locks had been changed. Cursing my stupidity, I had to be content with watching Amanda from afar. I was desperate to get into her bed, snuggle down into her duvet. The problem was I wasn't content, remembering the recording device I had put into her flat I sat and listened to the mundane everyday life they had together, rather than becoming bored I became increasingly jealous, why should he get to live the life with Amanda I so desperately wanted.

He could never give her all that I could give her, and he could never need her as much as I did. Meeting Lucy from work the week after my birthday I got my first long awaited glimpse of Amanda she had been absent from work on the first occasion I had gone to meet her due to her break in. I was resentful that I was being forced to spend so much time with Lucy just so I could get a glimpse of Amanda. When I finally saw, her I was awestruck, from my vantage point in the shadows I could see the weight was falling off her she looked under duress and pale with worry. I wanted nothing more than to go to her and feed on her despair. Instead, I had to spend the evening with Lucy who was so desperate for my approval she spent the evening picking at some salad whilst telling me about some fad diet she was starting. Gritting my teeth to prevent a cutting response I had to compliment and flatter her in all the right places knowing she was the only key I had back into Amanda's life. Going back home after yet another unfulfilling tryst with Lucy I was forced to listen as Tim and Amanda made love.

I found I was practically steaming with anger. Tim should not be making love to Amanda it should be me! I was putting in so much ground work to get back into her life, and I was getting nothing back in return. I was physically aroused by their love making though listening to her mewing, remembering the feeling of her below me. Listening to his grunts of pleasure I recalled how skilful she had become with her tongue. For the first time in a long time, I no longer felt control, I was being led a merry dance by a stupid girl, and they both needed to be taught a lesson

Waiting across the road from Tim's office I had convinced myself I didn't need to hurt him in the physical sense to get my revenge. My fleeting idea of getting him to ingest some damaging pill was long ago put on the back burner. Instead, I was going to tell him about myself and Amanda; tell him the sordid details of how she came to me, tell him how she fucked me without a second thought for him. This is what I told myself, yet I had dressed in a dark tracksuit and hoody. I had purchased a blade for the conversation that was to follow. A decision swayed by hurt. I wanted them to hurt as much as me, seeing my opportunity, I picked up my pace, head low the sound of the street muffled by my hood. Racing towards him I braced for impact. Totally unprepared for my assault he did not try to defend himself. A quick jab and it was done. Stabbing at him as I passed. If he reacted, I did not wait to see it? Instead of continuing to race in the direction of the hire car I had parked a street away. Getting into the car, I looked down and see Tim's blood spray over my hands. I could have paid for someone to do this for me, but I needed to get my hands dirty. Most disturbing it felt good, it felt just. Amanda's rejection of me had caused this. Hopefully, the stupid bitch would learn, nobody said no to Mathew Mason. I was done playing games now I was going to claim her.

Burning my clothes and disposing of the knife I washed changed and made my way to Lucy's half an hour before Amanda rang for a lift to the hospital.

Knocking at her flat door I was so anxious, this would be the first time we had been face to face since we had had sex. She opened the door, and the first thing I noticed was the overwhelming smell of brandy. All my worries of it being awkward were pushed to one side when it became apparent just how distraught she was. She really did love the baboon, and her sorrow for him was written all over her face. Lucy helped her to the car, I carried her bag for her at the first opportunity I was going to take her keys with a bit of luck I could make my excuses, get a new set cut and put them back into her bag before she left the hospital. There was no way I was going to allow her to lock me out of her life again.

Getting to the hospital we were all relieved to see that had survived his ordeal, Amanda was so relieved she almost fell. I had the pleasure of catching her, and it truly was a pleasure. Holding her in my arms she felt tiny, I don't think she was aware of it too caught up in seeing her darling husband, but I settled my crouch against her stiffening instantly.

I wanted to put my hand inside her shirt and roll her nipples between my thumb and finger. I wanted Tim to see me too helpless in his hospital bed to stop me from bending his wife over and fucking her at the end of his bed. This was all going through my head as Lucy made excuses so we could leave and they could be left alone. Using the events as an aphrodisiac, I pulled Lucy into a stock room pushing her to her knees. Without ceremony, I unzipped my flies and put my engorged cock between her lips, I fucked her mouth filling it with hot salty seaman, and she did not object in fact she seemed pleased with herself no doubt assuming she was irresistible. Kissing her, I tasted myself on her.

"Go and wash your mouth out you dirty little bitch."

Instead of being alarmed by my comment she smiled and replied,

"Yes, daddy".

For fuck sake, she actually thought I would find that comment sexy. This woman really had no clue. Perhaps I could send her to my father as a treat that was the kind of thing I was sure he would enjoy.

Chapter 21

M.

I spent Christmas alone, I managed to convince Lucy I had a pre-existing arrangement with family and I was going away for a few weeks. The reality, I intended to get some work done. My offices were shut over the Christmas period giving me the opportunity to go in uninterrupted and do some preparation for the New Year's accounts, it was a well-oiled machine that rarely needed my input, but I like to cast my eye over the operation whenever I could get into the offices alone. Most of my work was done at night when the office was empty or at the weekend or holidays like now. My professionalism had been on the back burner lately since my obsession with Amanda had increased tenfold, but with her away and my recent intervention still having big ramifications I put her to the back of my mind and concentrate on reading spreadsheets and proposals.

I didn't believe in Christmas bonuses; instead, giving my staff a performance related bonus in January. I needed to look at my employee's files and cross reference their sales to determine what percentage bonus they would get. All very mundane but time-consuming all the same. Christmas day I had my head in a file when my phone rang, I had already spoken to Lucy feigning a nap whilst my family prepared dinner, checking my phone I see it was Mavel, I answered with a bit of trepidation

"Mathew Mason speaking, how can I help?"

"Mathew, it's Mavel, Merry Christmas."

"Hello Mavel, Merry Christmas to you too."

This was a fruitless conversation, and we both knew it, as a family, we never celebrated Christmas the last time Mavel had tried my father had thrown the tree we had spent hours decorating into the fire.

"What do you want Mavel, cut to the chase."

"Mathew, you need to come home, your father has taken a turn for the worse he has asked for you."

"I won't be coming to see him Mavel, the sooner that monster is dead, the better as far as I'm concerned!"

"Mathew please, that monster is your father don't be so rude, if I'm correct the apple doesn't fall too far from the tree does it, are you forgetting the broken girls you have brought to me for patching up? First, when you were a teen and not many people would blink an eye, but the last girl Mathew the one last year how old was she? Eighteen, nineteen?"

My response was blunt

"Sixteen."

"Ahh, right sixteen and I was given the task of patching her up because at fifty-one you just couldn't control yourself could you Mathew? Your father may be a monster, but he has made you in his image. I am fed-up with covering up for you two, your father is very ill he needs to see you if you don't come then I'm not above going to him with your little trysts, let's see how well you can stand on the moral high ground then, shall we!"

I couldn't help but chuckle

"Mavel, I didn't know you had in you, all these years and you have finally grown a backbone!"

Her voice altered slightly almost taking on a tone of authority.

"I have always had a backbone Mathew, it takes a strong woman to deal with you and your father, to know what hurtful, hateful things you are both capable of but to still love you, to still protect you, that's not something a weak person can do Mathew. I'm an old woman I have made many wrong decisions in my time, mostly to protect my brother. I regret many things, I regret that Heather suffered so badly that she saw death as her only escape, I wish every day I could change that, I will not go to my grave knowing your father never got his dying wish. You will come home Mathew; I Have made your old bed up I expect to see you tomorrow."

With that, she put the phone down, and for the first time in thirty-five years, I was going home to my father.

Arriving at my old family home, I was full of trepidation. I had left one night under the cover of darkness, a coward exit but the only way I knew I could get away if my father was aware of my plans he would never have let me go. I often believed he would want me dead than take the risk of his sins being broadcast. Yet he had never challenged Mavel's existence, never demanded such control over her as he did me, perhaps he knew that she would never tell.

For if she told surely, she would also be guilty, for years she witnessed the aftermath of his abuse, first to Heather and then in the later years to us both, she has seen first-hand the horrors he was capable of and not once to my knowledge had she tried to stop him. She would shake her head disapproving as she patched me up after one of his attacks, she would comfort Heather and hush her when her sobs became too loud. But never did she challenge him, her own brother was capable of such horrors towards her niece and nephew, she knew of these horrors, yet she never stopped him. In later years, she proved to be useful to me too, so conditioned was I to her non-judgmental ways, I would often have her embroiled in my wayward activities asking she assist if I had been a little too rough. Even on occasions taking a young girl to her house so I might use her spare room for unsavoury activities. Why? Why had she never spoke out and told me or my father our ways were wrong? Would I have been a different man if she had? It was only speaking to her on Christmas day that she portrayed any signs of not agreeing with our antics, referring to us as both monsters. If we were monsters, then what was she? Perhaps she was Doctor Frankenstein, and we were monsters of her design?

Knocking at the large front door, it was opened by Mavel.

"Good, afternoon Mathew, I'm glad you came."

I tried to appear neutral but my voice portrayed the anger I felt

"Did I have any choice Mavel, you seemed to make it clear yesterday that I hadn't"

Her eyes seemed to gleam with mischief as she formed a reply

"Hmm well no Mathew, you are right I left you very little choice, I would have gone to extreme lengths to get you here, I'm just glad there was no need to. Come in Mathew I will make us some tea."

Looking her over she seemed frailer than when I saw her last, older somehow.

"You don't look very well Mavel, is nursing my father taking its toll on you?"

"Mathew, your father's entire existence has taken its toll on me! He is the reason I am old and unmarried, I have no family to call my own, no husband no friends. He has been my curse my whole life, my curse, and my blessing. But you are right I am unwell. I am tired of Mathew; for almost fifty-two years, since the death of your mother, I have been at your father's beck and call, his time on this earth is coming to a close. I fear that I have failed in preparation for this, I'm certain that without him to look after my heart may well break."

It hadn't dawned on me just how reliant upon my father Mavel had been, her verbalising it this way had made it clear. She had not told a soul of his misdemeanours, his years of abuse because he was all she had, the only family she knew, and she would rather protect a monster than face life alone.

Looking around my old family home I was surprised to see it looked nothing like I recalled. The rooms had a more feminine touch, soft fabrics adorned the windows, cushions were scattered artfully about the seating area.

"It does not look how I remember it has father developed a skill for interior design since last we met?"

Mavel looked at me disapprovingly, she appeared to think whether she would chastise me for my sarcasm but decided against it.

"I have been living with your father for the past ten years, I decorated when I first moved in and on a few occasions since he even got his hands dirty helping to paint the walls and door frames. It needs doing again, but since your father became ill, we have not had the energy to start a new project. I may get someone in."

I was beginning to tire of the small talk, my nerves were on edge, and by being proactive on the attack I hoped to take back some kind of control,

"Where is he, Mavel, where is the old goat? Is he hiding in the back room deciding if I have grown too much for him to challenge, biding his time deciding if it's worth attempting one last beating before we part ways again?"

She looked at me then, truly looked at me a hint of humour in her eyes,

"Your father is ill Mathew, but he is still bigger and stronger than you will ever be if he chose to beat you, believe me, he would win,"

"Really Mavel at almost eighty?" "Yes, Mathew really, he is not here at the moment he travels for alternative treatment. He has been away for the entire holidays, I expect him back in a few hours."

Her words shocked me when she had proclaimed my father's illness, I had imagined him bed bound and frail, but she had painted a picture of a strong, able-bodied man. This provoked fear in me, fear I had a task to disguise.

"Mavel, you have yet to tell me what is wrong with him, why is he so ill he must see me yet not ill enough to have become frail?"

"Mathew is that fear I see in your eyes?"

She was mocking me, mocking the panic and worry which was winding back into my being the same feelings I locked away and swore to myself nobody would ever make me feel again.

"Mavel, I'm the first to admit my father scares me, can I clarify why? He would actively rape my sister and make me do the same for fun! That makes him evil Mavel, why wouldn't I be afraid?"

She had the grace to look ashamed, ashamed to have been mocking me knowing full well what type of horrors he was capable of.

"You're right Mathew, I'm sorry I shouldn't goad you, he leads you a pig's life, and your escape from him was the best thing you ever did, it's just such a shame he had already damaged you beyond repair."

"No Mavel, my father did not make me the way I am today, I will not credit him for anything, good or bad. You avoided my question, what is so wrong with that I needed to see him?"

She took a deep breath composing herself to deliver what she thought to be grave news, I, however, considered it a blessing.

"Your father has been unwell for many years Mathew, recently it had advanced and became more aggressive and full blown, your father had HIV Mathew, and it has now advanced to AIDS."

The enormity of what she said hit me like a spade, if I was not sitting, I believe I would have fallen,

"AIDS, when, how long."

"a long-time Mathew perhaps as far back as fifty years, one of the first cases, I don't suppose you recall, but he travelled a lot, he spent a lot of time in Africa once your mother died, it's believed he may have caught it there."

The room was spinning before me, I gripped at the table to ground myself worried I would tumble.

"Mavel, my father and I, we both shared Heather, does he think he was infected then? ""He does Mathew, and that's why he needs to see you."

The real reason he had asked to see me become apparent, he had one last wicked move to make in this twisted game he insisted on playing, I was nothing but a pawn, and with one well-timed move, he was going to bring my world crashing down on me.

"I can't believe it Mavel, surely if I was infected I would have had symptoms by now! I would have been unwell!"

Panic really began to set in, the realisation of what her revelation implied,

"I have a son Mavel, he is eight, if I was infected would he be at risk?"

I had so many questions none of which I believed Mavel could answer.

"A son Mathew, I never knew."

"I had no need to tell you, and definitely no need to tell my father. I am not a good man Mavel, but my son, he is pure, and he is beautiful, and I would never expose him to the sickening human being that is my father, and you Mavel, well you are just as sickening by proxy, aren't you?"

Straightening her skirt, she refused to meet my eye instead becoming preoccupied with non-existent creases.

"I'm sorry you feel that way Mathew, but I can fully understand your reasoning, I had a son too once you know, a son that your father never had the pleasure of being acquaintance with."

I didn't know what to make of this, I had no idea she had a child always assuming she was a spinster.

"What happened to your son Mavel?"

A sorrowful smile tugged at her corner of her lips

"I gave him away, the day after he was born. My heart shattered, but I knew I was doing the right thing by him."

I had many questions, when? Who was the father, how did she hide the pregnancy?

"I travelled to an aunt before I began to show, it was nineteen seventy you were about seven, the father? Well that's obvious isn't it Mathew, the father was the same man I had to keep him from, your father, my brother."

The silence seemed to bounce off the walls, could this get any more fucked up? I doubted it, so somewhere I had a brother, or perhaps not if he too was infected he may have met an untimely end. I was just so terribly sad that the only person that may have escaped unharmed was my father himself.

Still in shock at Mavel's revelation, I took my bag to my old bedroom, I had brought my overnight bag but did not intend to stay more than a few days, and I found my room to be repressive and stifling. I refused to be intimidated by this visit, but I couldn't help the uneasiness that settled in the pit of my stomach. Mavel had said that my father was still in reasonable health so was the only reason he brought me here really to as I suspected rub my nose in things, to confirm he still had a hold over me after all these years, time would tell I suppose all I could do now was wait for his return.

As a child, I often dealt with stress the only way I knew how I would sleep or at least Fein it to prevent my father's sickening games. Being back home I found my old coping mechanism returning, lying on my childhood bed I fell into a deep seemingly dreamless sleep.

Chapter 22

A.

Boxing day was upon us, and I was beginning to become a little stir crazy, I found Tim's parents difficult to tolerate for a long period of time, there was only so many afternoon naps I could Fake in an attempt to remove myself from their company. His mother's insistence on pussy footing around Tim was infuriating, under normal circumstances, he would acknowledge her overwhelming behaviour, and we would mock her together, yet now he seemed to relish it she was pandering to his every need and treating him like a child.

When I challenged her behaviour with her he shot me down told me I was being childish and crass, I mean crass really? He had never found me crass before. Yes, we are from different class backgrounds, but Tim had always poo-pooed the class system and rightfully so insisted we were equal, yet here he was questioning my opinion as though I was not worthy of making an educated judgment on his mother's behaviour.

 I'm not proud to admit that I may have pushed a little too far purposely causing an argument so that I could make my excuses and leave. Tim's younger brother had suggested we go to the pub boxing day but Tim still being vulnerable had declined, after our argument I had sought out Tim's brother and consoled myself with a large whisky, after all, it was Christmas. Under normal circumstances, I would have thought nothing of spending the day and evening in the pub, but I was acutely aware that this would cause a further rift in our relationship. The Tim which was currently lying on his mother's couch covered in a blanket was not my husband; he was not the big strong rugby player that I married. I needed to be supportive of him in sickness and in health. My getting shitfaced and going back to his parents' house was nobody's idea of supportive. Instead, I had a few more drinks with his brother and had a look around the local shops at the Boxing Day sales. The weather was bitter much colder than in London, so I treated myself to a cashmere scarf and some leather gloves in a matching colour. Once I was certain there was no sign of the afternoon's festivities I made my way back. Entering the room Tim faced me and turned his nose up in

Disgust. Whispering so I could barely hear him, and his mother was none the wiser

"For fuck's sake Amanda, you just couldn't help yourself, could you? You smell like a brewery!"

"I had a few but that was hours ago, Tim, I'm not drunk honest, I went into town to do some shopping."

"Well that's a few too many isn't it, you promised you wouldn't drink anymore Mandy."

I was angry with his lack of imagination he seemed to fall back on the same old argument, I bit my tongue rather than antagonise the situation further. I had to remain aware he had been through a lot and was feeling very unsettled, but I don't think I did wrong, I did not make a fool of myself or him; instead, I had shown restraint and come back as sober as I had been when I had left.

"I'm sorry you're angry Tim, you seem to be angry a lot lately, but I want you to know I'm sorry if my actions have upset you; that was never my attention. I'm going a little stir crazy here that's all I needed to get out I knew your brother was on the cross, so I went to meet him for an hour before going shopping. I will refrain from drinking if it's what you want; I'm sure I will be fine once we get back home; I just needed to get out as I said"

"I'm not sure you can refrain, Mandy! It doesn't matter where we are you will always find a reason to drink, you think I don't notice Mandy, but I do! Home is not the answer for you, in fact, I think going home may well make you worse. I know one thing Mandy, I'm not ready to go home, I'm in no rush I think I will stay here for a few weeks until I'm back on my feet if you feel you can't stand to be here with me. Well, to be honest that suits me your disdain for my mother is apparent on your face I don't think she would be able to turn a blind eye to it for much longer."

"What actually are you saying, Tim? Don't hide behind mummy's apron strings now, say it as it is; what do you want?"

"I want you to go, Mandy. I want you to leave me here for a few weeks, a combination of your behaviour today and my desire not to go back to the flat just yet mean I think you should go on ahead without me. I know you have work after the new year, and you can't get out of it. Go back to London go to work hopefully I will get a bit stronger with my mother's help then I will come back. Mandy whilst I'm away I need you to think about what you really want, though! Is it me and a family or is it the ladette lifestyle you obviously led before I met you?"

I was struck dumb; it had barely been a month since the last "break" two in as many months did not make for a successful marriage. I found I wasn't as hurt as the last time; though I didn't feel so brittle and abandoned, he had been difficult to live with these last few weeks. I found I looked forward to the idea of being alone for a while, for so many years I had been alone with no one to answer too I found slipping into the wifey role a little more demanding than I had expected.

"Fine, Tim, I will pack and leave today, could you drop me to the station?"

"I'm not sure I can Mandy, but my Father can."

Looking at him I felt a shift something in me changed I still loved him dearly but I lost a little respect.

"Can I ask why you can't take me, Tim? I was hoping to keep this between us, involving your father would only bring up unnecessary questions."

"Mandy I can't I don't think I can be out after dark at the moment I'm sorry."

What could I say to that? , he had recently been stabbed for crying out loud, and he was still fearful, but in my eyes, he needed to get back into the saddle and sooner rather than later. My only hope was that his mother could succeed where I had failed and helped him fix his wounded soul.

"Okay, I will go and pack up."

He nodded in agreement, when I came back down with my bag, he was nowhere to be seen instead I was greeted by his father with his car keys in his hand.

Chapter 23

M.

The door creaking alerted me to someone in the doorway before I opened my eyes I made a wish for Mavel and not my father. Even after all these years, he instilled terror in me. Fifty-two and afraid of my daddy. I was not prepared to let this go on for much longer, I had removed myself from this situation many years ago, I was not about to be sucked back in like nothing had changed. I was not that boy anymore I was a man, a strong, confident, successful man I would not let my father take that away from me.

"Are you awake Mathew? It's tea time, and your father is home."

It was Mavel but she was not bearing good news

"Yes, I'm awake give me a moment to clean up, and I will be down, and Mavel"

"Yes."

"How is he? What kind of mood I mean?"

"He is in good spirits Mathew; the dark moods are a thing of the past he is a different man to the one you remember much mellower."

Mellow really? I would describe him as many things but never mellow. Gathering up my thoughts and confidence I started the journey down the narrow staircase. Entering the room, I was faced with my father, my nemesis. He stood as I entered the years I had spent away did nothing to dull the sheer dominance of his presence, he had lost weight since I have seen him last, but still, he stood at six foot four and easily seventeen stone, he seemed almost twice my size and width. I found I had to draw on years of acting to not appear afraid. He spoke first.

"Matti, I'm so glad you came home, it couldn't have been easy for you, thank you."

Composing myself further I replied.

"Given the choice, I wouldn't have, but Mavel had a few tricks up her sleeve. It seems I have a few angles that can be exploited and I'm afraid she did that"

I felt strained speaking to him, I was not sure I could recall any conversation between us before that was not strained. Had we ever had a normal conversation without fear or manipulation I wasn't sure we had.

"Sit Matti, I won't keep you longer than I need to, I will get off my chest what I have to say then you are free to leave."

He couldn't say fairer than that I suppose and I have to admit I was eager to find out what he wanted me for, why he had suddenly summoned me.

"As you know Mathew I am not a well, man, this illness is finally getting the better of me, I will not insult your intelligence by requesting your forgiveness, that is something I fear I may never be entitled too. What I am offering you is a chance for revenge. I have been an evil man in my time very evil as you well know. I cannot apologise as the part of me that tells me my actions were wrong is the same part of me that tells me given the opportunity I would commit those same sins again. One thing I have come to realise as I get older is there are many types of people in this world. I fall into the category that most would consider evil, I thrive on the bad things you see son if I was younger and fitter I would have a trail of victims. Those victims serve to feed this evil side. I will not apologise for something I feel no sorrow for! I am of course saddened that we could not have a "normal" relationship even someone such as me can see that "normal" is something that we all aspire to; perhaps if I were normal, I would have a daughter and a son who visit me once in a while. I might even have a few grandchildren perhaps I could buy them sweets and bounce them on my knee, hahaha, his laugh sent a shiver down my spine. He was offering no apology merely using evil as an excuse! I wasn't sure how I felt about this confession, it was nothing but honest.

"You are probably wondering why I have called you back home. It's not just to profess my sins Matti; I know I'm going to hell. I'm grateful for it. At least with me in hell, your mother and Heather would be safe from me. Do you believe in heaven and hell son?"

"No just good and bad, and you are definitely bad!"

He nodded in agreement

"Yes, I know, as I was saying now is your chance for revenge, I have a gun in my safe it belonged to my father. What I am asking of you is that you end my life, it cannot be traced back to you if you like I will stage it to look like a suicide. An eye for an eye Matti, your chance to put to bed all the bad feeling between us. Let's eat now your Aunt Mavel has prepared a nice meal, you can tell me your decision tomorrow morning, sleep on it, weigh up the pros and cons. I have been well enough recently to dig my own grave out on the land I have tied up my affairs if I was to disappear the only person that would miss me is Mavel, as you well know her silence goes without question."

I couldn't believe what he was asking of me, many a night I had lain in bed dreaming of killing him, hitting him with a car like I had Nate, stabbing him even shooting him and now he had offered it to me on a plate, I ate my dinner in silence, a beef wellington with all the trimmings under different circumstances it would have been pleasant. After dinner to avoid small talk I retired to my room, wide awake due to the sleep I had earlier in the day I attempted to read, what I really wanted to do was research. I wanted to research the probability of killing someone and getting away with it. However, I knew that would be silly it would leave evidence in my search engine.

Once I tired of trying to keep track of the book I was reading, I sat to consider my father's proposal. As with most things related to my father I had to question his true motives. Was it a cunning ploy to get me arrested perhaps so that he had the last laugh, I thought not, Mavel would not let that happen. The more I thought about it, the more this whole idea seemed to be stemming from Mavel, perhaps she thought revenge would be enough for me to move forward. She had expressed concern that my birthday celebrations continued in vein, maybe she believed with my father terminated, and by my own hand, it would be enough to help me move on? Maybe it would, I had tired of the call I received from the dark side, more than anything I wanted to participate in "normal" just as my father had said. I could probably sustain normal with Amanda in my life she was the only person I have ever truly felt I could make that leap with.

Maybe terminating my father and getting my redemption I could start a new life myself and Amanda, perhaps we could have a child together. Why couldn't I have happy, I deserved it too after all I had been through didn't I? Or had my sins against humanity counteracted my right to happiness? I weighed up many scenarios in my head that night finally going to sleep at two AM, my decision made. At the earliest opportunity, I was going to kill my father. I was going to destroy his physical body the same way he had destroyed Heathers, and most importantly I had decided I was going to enjoy it.

A.

The flat was cold when I got home all the lights were off, it felt weird returning with all the Christmas décor still in place, Christmas was over now, the unusual effort I had made to celebrate it this year had gone to waste. For the short time, we had been away the tree had taken to shedding most of its needles.

 First things first, I was no longer in the mood for celebration. I started by taking the decorations off the tree, taking care to wrap the delicate ones in tissue paper before putting them back in the box. Surprised by my own optimism. If I was going to use them next year, everything would have to be fine? No death by dangerous driver no stabbing, no brake in. I have had my fair share of tragedies surely now it was due to a good hand. Perhaps even next Christmas we would have our own baby? Come to think of it I was very late for my period, I had done tonnes of tests all negative. I googled it and whilst it rare to have a positive and not be pregnant it's quite common to have a negative and be pregnant. Why else had my periods stopped? It would explain my lack of appetite as well. As much as I dreaded facing the doctor once the New Year was out the way, I would need to book a blood test. Putting the decorations away proved to be the easy bit, getting the tree down into the communal bins was no mean feat.

 I tried pushing but got stabbed with so many needles I opted for pulling, there was a trail from the flat all the way to the bins of a dead tree. Starting at the top of the stairs I swept all the way to the bottom creating a sizable pile at the end. The flat was a different story. It turns out them needles are barbed little bastards I couldn't get them out of the carpet by hovering alone; instead, I sat having to pick them out individually. By the time it was done, it was late my back ached, and I was ready for my bed. I barely had a chance to miss Tim before I fell into a deep sleep.

The next day I couldn't say the same, with no work to endure, I pottered around the flat for a while unsure of what to do with myself. Ringing Tim to see how he was feeling I was met with his answer machine, hoping he just hadn't charged it as oppose to ignoring me I tried Lucy instead. She answered on the second ring.

"Morning Mandy, how are you, sweetheart?"

"Hmm not so good to be honest, I don't wanna go oh poor me on you, so I will keep it short, Tim's got the arse with me for some reason or another. He has stayed on at his mum's, and I'm back in London, do you wanna meet up for a drink? Maybe discuss something other than my miserable life? That's if you're not doing something with Mathew?"

"I'm free but do you think going for a drink is a good idea babe?"

I could tell from her tone she was saying this for my benefit, Lucy without Champagne is like Torvil without Dean

"Oh, for fuck's sake Luce don't you start; I will have a few shandies and be on my best behaviour now come on I have a husband to try to forget!"

"You don't want to forget him, Mandy, not with them buns! Ha ha ha"

"no, your right he does have a good arse, maybe I will remember that bit later when I'm home alone, it's one thing not having to put up with his sulking, but I miss the sex when he insists on these little retreats of his! Will I meet you at the brewery at about one? "

"Yep okay at the carpark side?"

"Yes, see you then."

With a few hours to spare, I decided to have a room change around. Since the break-in, the TV was in a different position, I liked it and thought it would be easier to see if I moved the chairs around a bit.

Going out into the bitter cold, I stood and waited for Lucy to arrive; a parade of sale shoppers passed me by. Once Lucy arrived, we made our way to a fast food joint to fill our bellies before we went drinking, neither of us was overly hungry and instead we settled on a muffin, once Lucy had removed her layers of clothing to protect her from the cold; I noticed she looked a little thinner

"How you been Lucy? You look like you have lost a bit of weight."

"Good thanks, yeah just a few pounds toning up more than anything, forget about me though Mandy, you look tiny have you had no luck gaining weight?"

"no I wish, it just seems to be falling off, I just don't seem to have much of an appetite at all, my size sixes are feeling big now which is awful this is the smallest I've been for years."

"Maybe try eating little and often, it may help?"

"I wished I could but every time I do eat it seems to go straight through me."

"You need to get it sorted Mandy, get onto the Docs it's not normal."

"I know I have an appointment booked for next week anyway I will mention it. God, I feel like I'm falling apart, nothing seems to be working properly at the moment, but you know what with the stabbing I have hardly had time to worry about myself."

"How is he? Is he bearing up?"

"to be honest Lucy I'm not sure he is, I tried ringing him today, and I'm pretty sure he put the phone down on me, I think he may need some kind of counselling, his physical wounds are healing nicely I wish I could say the same about the mental ones. His confidence has been knocked for six. He is currently holed up at his mums in the middle of nowhere, at the moment I think he would be content to never have to mix with people again, he is just so fearful. Don't get me wrong I completely understand why and I'm there for him I really am, but he just doesn't seem to want my help. It seems the more I try, the more he pushes me away. I'm fearful, to be honest, Lucy, I really hope we can get through this but the harder I try to get through to him the more he retreats."

"I'm sure he will come around he has been through a lot, more than anyone should have to deal with, how have the police got on do they have any lead? Surely with someone caught he will be able to sleep more easily?"

"Nothing, Tim seems to think the break in and the stabbing are related but seeing as I left the door open and there was no actual break in, the police aren't making a connection, they put up one of those serious incident boards where the attack happened, but so far no one came forward. They seem to believe it was some kind of gang initiation thing and Tim was unlucky and caught in the crossfire. Such a terrible world we live in Lucy!"

"God I know it's awful what happened to Tim, I know we all say it, but it couldn't have happened to a nicer bloke he never deserved that not in a million years. The last thing I would want to see happen is your relationship suffer as a consequence."

"I hope not, I love him so much but right now he is so hard to live with, I know its selfish but perhaps a break is what we both need a few weeks so we can miss each other. How is your love life treating you, did you see much of Mathew over Christmas?"

As soon as I asked I was filled with guilt, it was traitorous of me to ask him.

"No, he was with family, to be honest, I'm not too sure we have much of a future. I find him a bit, I don't know, mean, is that the right word he can be a little cutting sometimes. It's not so bad if I'm getting the opposite as well, but he doesn't seem to be as committed to us as I would like. I'm getting older Mandy I can't afford to piss a few years away on a relationship that's going nowhere."

"Yeah, I see what you're saying, this early into a relationship you should be all hearts and flowers if you are already having doubts perhaps he isn't the man for you?"

"No, I'm not sure he is, I will give it a few weeks, if things don't improve then I'm offski. Literally I've booked a skiing holiday the middle of Jan with my brother and sister in law; I was thinking of inviting him but at this rate I will be going alone. Off-grid and out of contact perhaps he will get the hint, I hate dumping people! Come on I need a drink too much sombre shit for my liking where do you wanna go?"

"I'm not fussy shall we try, Yates?"

Yates was busy for the time of day, but we managed to grab a table, the hustle and bustle were a lot to take in at first, music playing in the background and a raucous group of blokes that seemed to be playing some kind of drinking game in the corner. A few cocktails later and the noise didn't seem to be such a problem Lucy had managed to get into a conversation with one of the blokes from the crowd, and he was making googly eyes at her boobs. Checking my phone, I had missed three calls from Tim. cursing myself for missing his call I made my way outside to call him back. The phone rang as I was giving up hope for him to answer he answered with a curt hello

"Tim, it's me, sorry I missed your call "

"Yeah you did."

"I'm sorry, how are you feeling?"

"Where are you, Mandy."

"Erm, I'm out with Lucy, I met her in Romford, a bit of retail."

The lie came so easily.

"You should be careful Mandy; I don't like the idea of you being out and about."

Swallowing down the sarcasm that bubbled just below the surface I made a mental note to appease him as best I could.

"I'm fine Tim we won't be out much longer then I'm going home, my credit card can't take much more punishment." "Still I don't like the idea of you out in a crowd."

"I know Tim, I understand it makes you nervous, but the chances of anything happening to me are slim. How are you feeling is your mum looking after you well?"

"Yeah, I'm feeling better but it's only been a few days, I thought I would stay for a few weeks longer."

There was a question left in the air between us as though he was seeking permission from me.

"If you feel it will aid your healing maybe you should, Tim can I ask, are we okay? I know lots went on but are we okay?"

"He hesitated a bit longer than I would like

. "Yes, Mandy, as well as can be with your problem."

My problem, my hackles rose, but I was conscious of not antagonising him further.

"Well I am addressing them, Tim, maybe once you come home we can go somewhere together, talk through our issues."

"are you taking the piss Mandy, I have been brutally attacked, any issues I have related to the attack, I'm within my rights to play up a little, you, on the other hand, are just a piss head!"

His words hurt, I was fuming but the irony of where I was, was not lost on me.

"I'm sorry you feel that way Tim, but your idea of a piss head and mine are two different things, I have always been a social drinker I don't consider it as much of a problem as you do. But I'm controlling it for your sake more than mine. I'm doing it because I love you. I want us to work, I'm committed to us, Tim, and I just need to know you are?"

"I am Mandy I'm sorry, I'm not myself my head is really screwed up right now!"

"Do you want me to come and visit? We can go out get something to eat?"

"I think it's best if you don't to be honest."

I was a bit thrown by his response but wasn't sure why? It had only been a few days ago, he had asked me to leave so why was I surprised he didn't want to see me.

"Okay well let me know when you are ready to see me."

Asking permission to visit my own husband was not my finest hours. Even more distressing was him declining. This meant I was now in a pretty sour mood.

"I will call you in a few days Mandy."

"Okay I love you."

"I love you too."

With that the line went dead, turning back into the bar I ordered a large JD. This girl was not in the mood for sobriety today. Once Tim was home I was going to have complete abstinence, for now, I was going to enjoy my freedom.

M.

I woke earlier than usual making my way down to the kitchen, my father was absent, but Mavel was nursing a cup of tea.

"Morning Mathew, how did you sleep."

"Quite well considering, how about you?"

"I've had better nights, to be honest, your father tossed and turned most of the night, I wasn't sure if it was the fear of you agreeing to shoot him or refusing, but it disturbed his sleep which in turn disturbed me."

It all began to add up, and her slip disgusted me

"Sorry Mavel, am I assuming right? Do you share a bed with my father? Your brother? Is that not a little fucked up?"

"You're not in a position to judge Mathew, are you?"

"Oh, I think I can judge here Mavel It's definitely not okay!"

"It was different between me and Heather that monster forced me, I was a child, and he beat me black and blue so I would perform to his sick desires!"

Defensive Mavel was mean! Pulling back her shoulders she barked her response

"The other girls Mathew did daddy force you then too?"

I was fuming with her, all these years I believed she looked out for me, seeing my father as the monster he was, but here she was admitting to bedding down with him.

"Come, Mathew let's not argue please."

Looking at her I saw her for what she was, yet another victim my father had created. She might not see it now, but his poison had woven itself into her soul and rid her of her ability to see the difference between right and wrong.

The morning past quickly the atmosphere between myself and Mavel was strained, but she attempted to make small talk. It was mid-afternoon before my father put in an appearance.

"Good afternoon, how are my two favourite people?"

He leant in to kiss Mavel's cheek as she offered it up to him, I felt sick to the pit of my stomach Bile rising in my throat. Being in the room with him reminded me just how much I fucking hated him, just how much he had destroyed any chance I had of growing up normal, just how much I yearned to end his miserable existence.

"I won't beat around the bush Mathew have you made a decision?"

Startled by his lack of small talk I was caught unaware and reverted back to an age-old habit I had long ago grown out of.

"Ye ye ye ye ye yes, I ha ha ha ha ha have."

Angry and confused by the return of my stutter I felt my cheeks burning up as shame took over me.

"Ahh I see little Matti has made an appearance, how are you, dear boy? I must admit I had missed you; I was a little disappointed yesterday when I was met with such a cold, guarded figure of a man, I much prefer you when you are so broken you can barely speak."

He had the liberty to smile at his own comment. I was so angry I struck out with my fist. What would have been a blinding left hook had it made contact was instead another status symbol of my father's strength and authority. His reflexes had not dampened over the years, and he caught my fist in his.

"Matti, please not in front of Mavel, you have your chance of comeuppance just as soon as you have that gun in your hand, now I will ask you again, take your time before answering, form your words properly before you try to speak, have you made a decision?"

Standing as tall as my limited height would allow my back straight and a note of steel in my voice I replied.

"Yes father."

I spat these words as though they burnt my mouth.

"I have made a decision; I will fucking destroy you just like I have always dreamed of, and then I intend to dance on your fucking grave!"

I heard a sharp intake of breath from where Mavel stood if my father was surprised by my language he showed no sign merely nodding his head.

"Good, I'm glad you have taken me up on my offer. I hope that by doing this, you can find a way to move on from all the wrongs I have caused you. I will eat lunch and then proceed with things if that's okay with you?"

Another sharp gasp from Mavel; she had covered her mouth with her hand and was looking from my father to me.

"Already Ray, tonight must it be tonight."

"Yes Mavel, I won't keep Matti any longer than needs be."

She nodded in agreement. I had not put a timescale on events but tonight worked for me I was eager to get back to London back to Amanda, I was eager to wipe my slate clean cleanse my sins and start my new life with her. The life I deserved.

We ate in silence a grand meal even by Mavel's standards. A feast of all my father's favourite foods. He ate slowly savouring every bite. His last supper. Once he had finished eating Mavel made a big show of tidying away taking twice as long on every activity as though she wanted time to completely freeze. I was unsure of her motives what was the etiquette anyway? Was it bad manners to commit murder if the meat dish wasn't clean?

Shortly before seven my father stood,

"Are you ready Matti boy?"

Was I ready? His words caused me to shake uncontrollably. I don't think I have ever been more afraid, not when I had run into Nate not when I had stabbed Tim, not when my father had beat me to a pulp never. Why was I so afraid was it because it meant the end? The end of every excuse I had ever used for my behaviour. Without him here to blame maybe I was solely responsible for my actions; that scared me. I needed to use this as a means to cleanse myself, after this I would have to be good; otherwise, I was just as rotten as he was.

"I'm ready father come let's get this over with I'm eager to get away, the stench from your rotten decaying body is causing me to sicken."

It was a low blow, but I was over caring. We made our way to the back room my father went to a cupboard and produce a pair of latex gloves and a gun, I'm not a gunman, but I knew it was a pistol. He handed the gloves to me and then the gun. It was heavier than expected it felt solid in my palm. Looking at my father he had the grace to look a little unnerved.

"Where shall I stand? This is not the sort of thing I have contemplated before, where would I like to stand for my death? Mavel, my love, I suppose it's up to you where is it easier to clean the blood stains from?"

Mavel merely shook her head tears flowing down her cheeks as she attempted to mute the sobs escaping from her mouth.

"Matti, Mathew thank you for agreeing to do this for me, could I just say."

BANG, he would not just say anything this was not going to be on his terms. The shot was a good aim seeing as I had never fired a gunshot into his head had delivered the bullet into his left eye. I had intended to shoot him between the eyes, but the lack of practice meant my aim was off. His body did not fall straight away instead swaying as if deciding if it was really dead or not. My ears rang out with the shot. The ringing in my ears was broken by Mavel's screams she ran to him. His body motionless on the floor she lay across him as his blood seeped from the open wound. Putting the gun down I removed the gloves put them into my pocket and left the room, retrieving my bag from my room I left got into my car and drove away not daring to look back. As I drove away, a bang rang out, it barely registered in my addled brain, my car may need looking at if it was backfiring.

Getting back to my country house I took a hot bath and fell into bed to shock to feel a thing. Waking the next morning the memory of the previous day's events plays like a film reel through my head. My father's body making its final descent to the floor Mavel's shocked face as she ran to him. My own hands shaking as I removed the latex gloves, going to my jacket pocket I took out the gloves and chucked them into the wood burning stove. I heard the faint sound of the letter box signalling the postman delivering my letters. Going to the door I was surprised to find a handwritten letter addressed to Mathew Mason, most of the post I had sent to this address had the company name on them. Opening the letter, I see it was signed off by Mavel.

Mathew,

By the time, you receive this letter, you would have completed the task your father had asked of you, I am sending this letter so you may be a bit better informed than you were previously.

Your father has indeed been rather unwell for a while. However, it was not AIDS as I previously stated. He had insisted I stick to this story so further to feed any hate you may have toward him; I would have left you in the dark about this had it not been our conversation about you having a son. I don't want you to worry unnecessarily, I was surprised you bought it at all as it is my understanding AIDS did not come to the western world until the mid-seventies. Your father was, in fact, showing the signs of Alzheimer's. He was getting worse on a daily basis. He had decided to end his life as soon as he realised he was only going to deteriorate. He had done some research of course; he had wanted to travel to Sweden, but it was so expensive Mathew he couldn't possibly afford it. Whilst he had no trouble asking you to kill him as a way of revenge he was not happy to ask you for money. You know your father he is as stubborn as you are in that respect. Of course, he asked me to do it at first, he did not want to have to ask anyone for help being such a proud man. But I couldn't Mathew I couldn't do that last thing for him. I love him too much you see. I would do anything for your father, even give up my own child but I could not destroy him, I could not end my time with him, not by my hand. I helped him, though, together we came up with a plan to get you to help. He was telling the truth when he said it would help you move on, help you get the redemption you deserved. If I could have one wish Mathew, it would be to wish you were unscathed by your father's wicked ways. It would be that you have a happy, fulfilling life.

Now your father's life has ended you have no need to be associated with us again. Hopefully, you can move forward reborn as a new better person. I, however, cannot do the same, your father was my life you see, whilst I was unable to end his life. However, I am in no doubt without him to love mine is not worth living. As soon as I can, I will join your father in hell and try to keep him out of trouble

My deepest love, gratitude, and apologise that I could not stop the torture you and Heather endured,

Aunty Mavel

X x X

Perhaps I should have been upset by her confession, but my father's story was as close to honest as he could afford. I did not feel hoodwinked or cheated, instead, I felt relieved. Relieved my son was safe, relieved that Amanda and I were free to live a long and happy life together and if she agreed we could have a child of our own a healthy beautiful baby. I really did feel reborn the time for lies and manipulation was coming to a close.

I was almost ready to make Amanda realise that she needed me as much as I needed her. I just needed to get Tim out of the way. I was angry that my previous attempt had been unsuccessful, the stab wound had missed all major organs; some guys have all the luck! I couldn't make another attempt on his life it would be too much of a coincidence. There was no point in me getting Tim out of the way only for me to end up in prison and not get to spend any time with Amanda. No, I had to be clever here I needed to win her fair and square. The old me, the me that mirrored my father may have thought of a manipulative way to win her, but I was eager to move forward as a good person with a healthy mind. I only hoped I could do so quickly because now more than ever I needed the calming sedative that only Amanda could offer. In fact, come to think of it, my whole body was alive with electric each nerve ending buzzing like a current was running through them. Normally when things were this bad, I would have had no choice but to visit Amanda's flat lie upon her bed but I was a better man now I was going to try my best to control the chaos running from the tips of my fingers to the ends of my toes.

A.

The evening out with Lucy turned out to be good even after taking a negative spin due to Tim's paranoia, once I returned to the bar after my phone conversation Lucy was well and truly the Centre of attention for the younger crowd. At first, I was horrified the idea of vying for her attention over a group of twenty-somethings was not something I was looking forward too. However, they were a nice group of lads. I had to stifle a laugh when one of the boys made reference to Lucy and his mum in the same sentence. Safely moved into the mum zone, we spent the evening acting as agony aunt as each of them presented us with a problem only the mature would know the solution too.

A few drinks and a whole load of stress release later I went home merry and slightly fuzzy but far from drunk. I had worked for a few days before the New Year's celebration this meant I had little time to miss Tim. I had plans to go to my sister's new year's, she had been on at me for years to go, but I always managed to find an excuse. Tim had insisted I take her up on her offer he said the idea of me with a bunch of strangers in a random bar was too much for him to bare. He wanted me safe, surrounded by family was as safe as I could be. The idea of being in a room with my mum after all these years was not something I looked forward too, in fact, I had actively avoided it for the past four years. On the few occasions, our paths did cross a polite nod was given.

One thing I did have time to do in Tim's absence was thinking; I mulled over the breakdown in the relationship between myself and my mother. I was mostly to blame, but my pride had stopped me so many times from healing the rift. It got to the stage where it was left so long it became too big to heal. Not really remembering why we had fallen out but knowing it was monumental at the time. Sitting in my flat missing Tim, I began to explore the importance of a loving family. I resented the relationship that Tim had with his mother could it be I was jealous? It had been so long since I had spent time with my mum I found their relationship a little unnerving, but this was my issue surely? I was finding the most natural bond between mother and son unnerving. Perhaps now it was the time I made an effort to heal the rift between my mother and myself, with the prospect of my own child on the horizon suddenly having my own mother back in my life felt very important to me.

I caught the early train back home to my sisters. It was a journey I made a few times a year yet every time it still managed to provoke the same reaction. The journey involved a few train changes and a couple of hours in total. Every time I returned home or travelled back to London the same feelings overwhelmed me. The feeling of being eighteen and confused, eighteen and having lost my way. Which is ironic as at eighteen I had the world at my feet yet I felt so broken so soiled, my self-worth was at an all-time low I felt I was good for nothing. I took that train having exhausted every avenue with my mother.

My sister tried to support me, but she had two young children of her own she couldn't allow a drunken, thieving mess like me to be such a major distraction from her main job which was raising her girls. She tolerated so much more than she should ever have and for that reason, I will always be grateful. Fortunately, my nieces don't recall much of that era instead choosing to remember me as the cool aunt who would lavish gifts and fun days out upon them whenever I visited. As far as I can make out my sister never shared the less savoury stories of that time with my nieces. They are none the wiser to the endless boys I brought home in desperation to feel loved. They have no memory of me falling through the door so drunk that I couldn't walk. I'm pretty certain Lacy doesn't remember me being sick in her dolls pram. I'm reminded of all these things as the train gets nearer to home as the houses thin out and make way for country fields.

The church tower that is seen from the window signals I'm nearing my destination, and I'm always grateful at this point that I'm still here to make this journey. My bad patch only lasted six months, but during that period I almost died on two occasions, once when I od on a bad batch of whizz and another time when I almost choked on my own vomit. Both occasions my sister like my own guardian angel was there to save me. I've heard of some of the group of people I hung around with not being so lucky, my old boyfriend James for example after he was caught selling drugs his plans for university and a career in economics where squashed instead he made a living as a small-time drug dealer. His career choice had a few negatives, but I don't for a minute think he would have factored high-speed police chases into his schedule. One such high-speed chase resulted in a nasty crash with a lamppost James never stood a chance and was killed instantly. He was twenty-five. I was thankful I had chosen not to continue any relationship with him as chances are I could have been sitting at home waiting for him on that night.

Shaking off the melancholy feeling provoked by coming home I decided I was going to enjoy my time. I should come back more often I loved spending time with my sister, my nieces were the apple of my eye. When the girls were younger, their dad was sent to prison, instead of choosing to wait for him to come out my sister had decided she wanted better for her girls. She spent years at uni and training whilst mum watched the girls, qualifying as a teacher. She distances herself from Dale. She had done so well in her chosen profession she was now a head teacher. She had the best of both worlds having had the baby's young she still managed to do really well for herself, and I was so proud of her. Disembarking from the train, I was met with a beep beep. My niece Lacy was driving a little fiesta a p for pass plate situated on the bonnet.

"Hello stranger, how are you? Nice wheels' congratulations on passing your test, although if I'm honest, I would much rather mummy had come to pick me up!"

"Aunty Mandy you have no faith in my driving skills! I passed didn't I! Anyway I have a late Christmas present inside for you be nice, and I will let you in."

Getting into the car, I was a bit nervous. I had never passed my own driving test, but I considered myself to be an expert on driving, one of them people that give constant commentary on other people's driving, "bit fast, too close to that car, late braking" that type of person I believe another name for us is annoying. I wasn't looking forward to getting into a car with Lacey knowing she had only passed her test two weeks ago, with a bit of luck, the green p plates would mean other drivers would give us a wide birth. As she started the engine, I was delighted to hear the opening lines to cherish.

"Ahh, great taste in music I see!"

"It's not mine it's for you, I thought you might enjoy listening to it on the way back."

"Excellent choice, I would choose Madonna over the crap you listen to any day of the week."

"Mandy, you need to get with it girl you sound like you are about sixty, your only thirty, you're not past it yet, live a little listen to kiss once in a while!"

I had to smile at Lacey's comments sometimes I felt so old before my time. Not so much since being with Tim although sometimes I felt like his mum despite there only being a two-year age gap. At least I used too, where had my carefree immature sometimes idiotic husband gone? I missed that version of him. I made a mental note to call him as soon as I got to my sisters.

We needed to grab the bull by the horns I needed him back I needed the love and joy he brought to me. I had a kid myself I needed the break as much as he did but I was wrong. Without him, at home, I was pottering around in a dull fuzz. Everything seemed to be black and white, I wanted my coloured life back the one where every sense was alive the one where the sun was brighter and the smells stronger the noises he made as he slept like music to my ears. The question was, did I deserve him? Look how quickly I had jumped into bed with Mathew fucking Mason, how I had put the thought of my beautiful, perfect husband to the back of my mind just so I could try to heal an age-old wound.

Lacy spoke up interrupting my train of thought. "How is Tim Mandy, I was hoping he would have come with you."

"Not too bad, I'm going to ring him once we get to your mums. I'm hoping he will come back after New Year. I miss him a bit now, to be honest."

"I bet you do, not how you imagined spending your first new year together."

"no, not really."

Exhaling the sadness, I tried to perk up. I had been sad and depressed for too long with my help together we were going to fix Tim and bring him home back where he belonged.

Getting back to my sisters she met me at the door with eggnog,

"Mandy, look at you, you're so thin! What's going on are you not eating."

"I'm trying I really am, but the weight is just falling off, don't worry I have a doctor's appointment booked for next week. Hopefully, they will get to the bottom of it, how have you been?" "Good, good come in don't just stand there, Bob and June are inside they are eager to see you it's been years!"

"Bloody hell, Bob and June, I thought they had moved away, must have been twelve years easily."

The reunion with my aunt and uncle took up way too much of my time it was almost seven before I finally got the chance to give Tim a call,

"Hello, Tim how are you."

"I'm good, I feel better today, how about you? Where are you?"

"I'm at livs, remember I said I was catching the train down" "Oh yeah, how you been?"

"Okay, I'm missing you though Tim, this is not how I imagined our first new year's together."

My disappointment seemed to hang in the air between us "I know Mandy I'm sorry, I just couldn't face the idea of coming back to the flat, not after everything that's gone on."

"Well we need to deal with it Tim sooner rather than later I hate you being away, what should we do, shall I look at moving? Renting somewhere else? Somewhere you would feel safer?"

Whilst the idea had only just occurred to me, it seemed like a good solution.

"You love that flat Mandy, I couldn't expect you to do that."

"I love you more though baby, I need you back home, and to top things off I'm feeling soo horny! When do you think, you will be coming back?"

He laughed at my comment but sadly didn't respond in kind, perhaps he was with his mum and couldn't talk.

"I miss you too Mandy, keep talking like that, and you will be seeing me sooner than you think." There was a knock on my door, "just a second Tim, someone is at the door."

Putting him on hold, I went to open it, and there he stood, my beautiful bear of a man. Looking a little thinner than when I had last seen him, but he had that twinkle in his eye that had been missing for the last few weeks

"You bastard, what are you doing here?"

"blame Lacey, she telephoned yesterday and bollocked me for letting you spend our first new year alone, she just picked me up from the station, drives like a fucking loon and had me singing the whole way back!"

I was completely in shock so much so I couldn't help but cry

"Oh Tim, I've missed you so much come here."

Careful not to hurt him I went in for one of his infamous bear hugs. He smelt divine just like home so warm and safe.

"Are you coming back to me Tim, I mean it if you want we can move, we can stay in a hotel until we find somewhere I don't care where as long as I'm with you".

"If I wanna be spared your niece's raff I think I better. I'm so sorry for how I have been these last few weeks Mandy I have just felt so vulnerable. I needed a few days with my mum, I'm a grown man, but sometimes your mum is the only person that can fix things. I know you're my wife though and it's time I grew up a bit and acknowledged it doesn't matter how afraid I am cutting you out is not the solution."

Looking into is face as he laid himself bare to me admitting his fear; I felt so much love for him.

"Plus, there are a few things you can do for me my mum can't."

With a cheeky check over his shoulder to make sure we were alone he walked into the bedroom closing the door behind him,

"I've missed you wifey way too much."

With a practised hand, he had my bra undone before I realised, his mouth expertly found my breasts, I couldn't help but groan as the warm from his mouth spread between my legs.

"I've missed you to Tim but it's likely my mum is downstairs by now, I have a lot of making up to do the last thing I want to do is confirm her suspicions that I'm a hoe and a tart!"

This stopped Tim dead.

"Your mum thinks you're a hoe and a tart? Why the hell would she think that?"

I had forgotten that I hadn't explained my history in full to Tim, at our wedding I had managed to explain my mum's absence away. He had asked after her a few times concerned that he had never met her. I had told him our relationship was rocky due to my behaviour as a teenager. I hadn't gone into much more detail.

"It's a long story, Tim, I promise tomorrow once this party is over with I will sit down and explain. For now, can we just go down and put on a united front? We can finish this off later."

"Yeah, no problem, but how should we play this?"

"What do you mean?"

"Should I like your mum or am I to dislike her by proxy?"

"Ha ha, Tim if you like her then you can make your own decisions. My mum's option of me are not unfounded, she is a good person a nice person. It's just for a while, I was a bad daughter. Hopefully, I'm mature enough now to apologise, and we can move on from it. I admit I resented the relationship you have with your mother but only because I was jealous. I want that too, and if I can apologise tonight I'm hoping I can salvage something of what we have left."

"Right, well I'm intrigued to know what went on? But I can wait if tonight you want to make up with mummy then I'm there to help the best I can."

"Thank you, we can stay here tonight as soon as normal business resumes I will get onto an agency and see about moving okay? We can let ours whilst we rent and maybe sell and think about moving. Perhaps rent for a while and think about upsizing in preparation for a baby? That's if you still want one with me?"

"Mandy of course I do, but we both need to understand that there is some fixing to be done on both our sides. If a baby comes along during that time great but we do need some serious talking to take place along the way."

"Agreed, but for now let's face the music. Hopefully, we can welcome in the new year on a positive note."

Walking down the stairs I felt so nervous, the party was in full swing now I took a minute to get Tim a beer and myself a diet coke, scanning the room I looked for the formidable form that was my mother. I see her sitting and talking with an aunt, lifting my hand in a weak gesture I made my way over to her. My aunt must have been aware of our situation as she made short work of making space for me and becoming engaged in conversation with someone to her left.

"Hello mum."

"Mandy, hello."

Drawing Tim in, I introduced my husband.

"Mum this is Tim."

"Good to finally meet you at last, how are you feeling after the attack?"

I didn't know she was aware of it but obviously, Liv must have passed the information on.

"Better thanks getting there."

"Good, I need you fit to look after my daughter now she lives so far away from home."

She smiled towards me. Putting the empty space next to her. Tim to his credit read the situation correctly and excused himself so that we had a chance to speak.

"I will look after her that I promise, I'm going to get some chicken if you don't mind?"

Okay so ditching his mother in law in favour of chicken might not have been his finest hour but his intentions were good. I was startled when my mother took my hand into hers.

"It's so good to see you, Mandy, look at you all grown up and married. Very handsome he is too. You look happy, are you?"

"Yes, mum I am."

"Good, I've had updates from Liv over the years, and I'm sorry things went a bit wonky for you. You have no idea how much I wanted to call you when things were hard, but I wasn't sure you were ready."

I was surprised that my mother had skipped the small talk and gone straight to the elephant in the room

"You did? Even after everything I put you through?"

"Mandy, you were a kid, what happened was not your fault, I should have been there to support you more, but when you left, you were so angry. The few times I had seen you since you still seemed so mad at me. At first, I convinced myself you would come back once you forgave me, but as the years went on and you didn't make contact I lost hope."

"Mum what do you mean forgive you? It was me that was out of line I should never have treated you the way I did."

"Oh, Mandy honey you were so confused and hurting so much, I was a terrible person for not seeing that you needed me more than ever. I should never have thrown you out the way I did. I honestly thought you would stay with Olivia for a while, I needed a bit of a break from your antics that is all. I was going to bring you back home but that day I came to collect you was the day we had the big argument, do you remember?"

I nodded, how could I forget, it was the day I raised my hand to my mum, the day I decided I was big enough and ugly enough to do what I wanted when I wanted. I hadn't taken kindly to my mums interfering ways. Things had got heated, and I had swung a punch at her.

"Mum I'm so sorry for all the trouble I caused; I really hope you can forgive me. It's been too long I wasn't sure of what reception I would receive. I only wish I had tried to make peace sooner."

"You have nothing to be sorry for, if it wasn't for that dirty old bastard of a boss you would never have gone through so much. He broke your heart just so he could get his leg over. I hope it was worth it, twelve years I have missed out on your life because that stupid man broke you!"

I couldn't disagree. Why did it seem Mathew Mason was the route to all my problems? Here I was years later, and he still shook my foundations to the core. That man was toxic the further away from him I was, the better.

Chapter 24

M.

Despite my best intentions, I was struggling to stay away from Amanda's home. I had contacted Lucy we had made plans to spend New Year at an exclusive hotel in London. At this short notice, the tickets were elusive. I managed to track a couple down. She had let slip during our phone conversation that Amanda and Tim had gone to a party out of town. I decamped to my London apartment.

My intentions were honourable at first, I was going there based on the best location for our night away; however, knowing Amanda flat was empty was too much of a temptation. I was an hour's drive away. I would have time to go in there then go on to meet Lucy as planned. Showering before I left so I was able to get dressed once I checked into our hotel room I made my way to Amanda's.

I felt a little deflated that I had given in so easily, I was hoping the cleansing ritual I had completed at my fathers would have made me stronger, more able to resist Amanda's pull. Driving to Amanda's my mind was in overdrive. I do most of my thinking whilst driving it's as though the motion of the wheels are directly linked to the cogs in my brain. The first half of the journey I was berating myself for being so weak, I felt like I had no option but to be near her, the second half I was no longer in full control of my mind the closer I got to her home the faster my heart beat. Could it be that someone's body could be directly linked to another I wondered? Could being close to her, close to her belongings be enough to make my heart race of its own accord. Was I being a romantic assuming I was excited to be in her surrounding again or could it truly be that on a primal, animalistic level we were meant to be together? Somehow being in her home changed the way I functioned physically? Making me stronger, more responsive, and more positive. I arrived at her flat in less that forty minutes the usual rush hour traffic was not a problem as it was New Year's Eve. Under the cover of darkness, I made my way up.

Knocking at that door to ensure it was empty I tried the key. Relieved that the new set of keys had been cut correctly, I entered. Something seemed a little different looking around I noticed the furniture had been moved, but it was something else, not a physical difference but something else. Taking a deep breath, I allowed myself to feel close to her. Moving to her bedroom, I found an empty unmade bed. Lying down I breathed in the smell of her pillow. It was then I noticed the difference her bed smelt sweet and clean there was no evidence of her baboon husband having recently inhabiting it. Looking around the room, there was very little evidence he had been here recently. Apart from a framed photo of them both in the bedside cabinet, I felt only Amanda in this room. This excited me, the idea of her here alone at night sleeping stretched across the bed the way she used too. I have endless memories of watching her through a covert camera. Sleeping horizontally across her bed. I knew things about Amanda that Tim couldn't possibly know, how does he have the right to share her bed. I knew her probably better than she knew herself. I knew what was good for her and Tim wasn't.

I was going to take her as my own, and I intended to do it sooner rather than later. I lie back in her bed, and I'm ashamed to admit I found myself aroused by the thought of her alone, the thought of her defenceless and sleeping. I had tried so hard not to be consumed by these thoughts intent on trying to be a better man, but with Amanda, I knew only one emotion it was an overwhelming need. A need to have her to be with her and to be immersed by her. The years of obsession was threating to consume me. The sooner I started a legitimate relationship with her the better it would be for us both. I could be good for her together we would complete each other. I would gladly care for and support her in exchange for the serenity and satisfaction she could give me in return. Once again, I cursed the younger me, the version of me that had her in my grasps but was convinced life would be better without her. Sixteen years had been wasted. Sixteen years that I could have spent by her side. For so long I had convinced myself that I was the author of my own destiny, but I was mistaken. From the moment, I saw Amanda I was enslaved to her, tied to her with invisible strings. Being away from her had sickened my mind and my body. The power she held over me was stronger than anything I have ever had to deal with. Surely, she must feel it too, she wouldn't deny me much longer of this I was confident. Taking her pillow between my thighs, I rubbed my erect cock against it. I would not allow myself to orgasm.

There was still a strong possibility Lucy would expect me to fuck her tonight. Whilst here I would allow myself to get as close as could without getting a physical release I would enjoy Amanda's tiny, frail body again soon, but for now, I would have to be content with scraps of her life colliding with mine. I lay for a while longer painfully aware of my body straining for release. Time had run away with me, I had half an hour before I had planned to meet Lucy. Reluctantly I moved out of Amanda's room and back out into the cold night, I was going to try to enjoy tonight. A rare occasion where I would let my guard down, I was leaving the car at the hotel. Confident that next year was going to be my year I was going to have a few drinks and try to relax.

Reflecting on the closing year, I had a lot to be grateful for; business was booming, five years ago I had been made an offer from a larger company to buy me out, and I had refused. Early this year I had bought them out and doubled my portfolio. More importantly, I had finally gotten Amanda back in my life, my father was no longer an issue the worry and doubt I locked away regarding him had now been resolved, and to my satisfaction, it was by my own hand I had managed to end him. I was bullet proof, I deserved a treat maybe I would source some cigars it had been a long time since I indulged, but I deserved it this coming year was going to be my happy ever after.

All these years of uncertainty and living life on the sideline was coming to an end I was now ready to be reborn and live the life I always should have done. I was finally ready to publicly define myself. I was going to be Amanda's partner, together we would take on the world. We would tell antidotes about how we first met and how I broke her heart, but finally, I came to my senses and won her back. We wouldn't have to deny our feelings any longer I would shout it from the rooftops myself. Proud to finally have her back in my life where she belongs. I would have no shame in telling Tim and Lucy. I understand she would not want to hurt them, but surely, they would understand that it was destiny we should be together. Rich, powerful and content. No more sneaking around no more stolen moments and stealth observations. I was feeling on top of the world by the time I got to the hotel confident in my future.

Checking into our room, I dressed quickly, a tap at the door alerted me to Lucy's arrival. Opening the door I was impressed with what I saw, she had made an effort. She was a polished woman anyway, but tonight she looked dazzling. It felt only fair I complimented her on it. I was in a fantastic mood and felt like spreading the joy.

"Good evening Lucy, you look stunning, come on in"

She nodded at me as she entered the hotel suite.

"wow, this is special Mathew how did you manage to book this at such short notice?"

Pouring her a drink from the bar I took her a drink and helped to remove her coat.

"Money talks Lucy, it was booked for tonight, but a word in the right ear and compensating the person who was doubled booked with us handsomely meant I secured it."

Looking around I took in the surroundings for the first time since my arrival. The honeymoon suite it was larger than most rooms in this hotel. Plush curtains complimented the marble floors. A huge chandelier adorned the ceiling. It was bright and spacious and just a little OTT for my tastes.

"How was your Christmas Matti? I missed you."

She looked across her glass at me, and she asked making eye contact to try to portray her lust. Normally I would have been repulsed at such a blatant display, but tonight I would only see the positive. Picking up my drink I made my way over to her chair.

"It was good thank you, how about yours."

I kept my dialogue to a minimum I didn't want to discuss Christmas anymore I was ready to lock the events away. Her cheeks flushed, and I entered into her personal space, she appeared nervous. "Good yeah, I wondered if perhaps you had lost interest in our relationship, I had expected to hear from you more." Kneeling before her I rub my hands up her calf's

"I'm still interested, Lucy, you're the key to my future that excites me."

She responded to my touch by opening her legs slightly.

"That sounds interesting Matti, I've been called many things but never a key."

My hands moved further up her thighs cupping her sex through the fabric of her underwear.

"Hmm, well like I said it excites me."

She giggled at that point thrusting up towards my touch,

"I never took you as a locksmith Mathew, but if that's what you like I think my lock needs servicing it seems a little rusty."

She amused me. She was a humorous woman I was glad our paths had crossed. She made this process easier. I found fucking her was easier tonight I enjoyed the sensations her body brought me. I was pleased with myself for maintaining an erection and giving a good performance. We dress with ten minutes to spare before dinner was served.

"Lucy I have something for you, sorry it's late."

Reaching into my case, I pulled out a blue bag. I had bought it before Christmas as a sweetener. She had served me well and deserved a treat for her time. Her face lit up as she opened up the bag and took out a pair of earrings,

"Oh, Mathew they are beautiful, you shouldn't have"

At this point, I should have said they were beautiful like her or offered her some kind of compliment, but I was done with giving her false hope. I wasn't going to be hurtful towards her, but I no longer felt the need to offer her false hope.

"Let's go to dinner Lucy, I'm eager to start this New Year."

Kissing me on the cheek she looked at me as if seeing me for the first time, her expression was different to normal she looked at me as though she saw something that wasn't there before.

"yes, let's go thank you again for the earrings, if I don't get the chance later, happy new year Mathew, and remember to celebrate what you want to see more of"

"Wise words right there Lucy!"

"They are, but I cannot take credit, Tom Peters, an author, we share a birthday."

"Ha ha, I know him well, all the best business men have read in search of excellence, but I don't know his birthday."

"Let's not forget the best business women, his birthday as is mine is the seventh of November."

She had surprised me with her reading choices pleasantly so.

"Well happy belated birthday."

"Thank you, now come let's eat I'm famished".

The night went without a glitch beautiful woman on my arm meant my ego was stroked. Men looked on with envy in their eyes the drink was flowing and the angst I did not know I was withholding started to drain away. Midnight was met with singing and dancing. Strangers kissed each other and wish each other merriment and success for the future. For the first time, as far back as I could remember I was excited about what was in store.

The night ended around three. We fell into bed too drunk to consider anything but sleep. Unusually for me I never woke until ten, my head throbbed reminding me that I had drunk too much, but nothing was going to sour my mood. Lucy began to stir beside me. She peeled open her eyes. I opened the curtains, and Lucy groaned as the light hit her.

"You're not about to come clean as a vampire are you Lucy? I think I can see smoke."

"Ha ha, very funny Mathew the only smoke from me is coming from my feet, I danced so much!"

She picked up her phone and began scrolling through her messages. "Anything interesting?"

"Yes actually, a message from Mandy."

My ears pricked up at her name. Trying to remain unaffected I kept as calm as I could.

"Really, what's wrong?"

"Not much, she looking for a new flat her and Tim are moving, she wanted to know if I could contact an agent friend of mine."

"Moving? That's a surprise why that's?"

"I'm not sure to be honest probably due to the break in and Tim's attack, I can't say I'm too surprised."

Before I could think things through I blurted it out.

"I have a few properties in Havering that have just been refurbished if she is interested."

"Excellent, I will let her know."

She had tapped out the text before I had processed the implications of what I had just said. The flats in question were the very same that Amanda had moved to when she had left home. It was too much of a coincidence that I should now own them. Amanda was not a silly girl she would do the maths and realise I had owned them when she had lived there. I may have accidently shown my hand. It was a good job I no longer felt the needed to hide things from her. Maybe it was the time I came clean and told her I had always been part of her life.

Even the nights she cried herself to sleep, I was there watching over her. Maybe she didn't need to know I meant it in a literal sense. But it was true I had spent many nights watching her so sad and broken. Yearning to go to her and wallow in her pity with her. I wanted nothing more than to immerse myself in her tears. Coming clean was my plan now, but even I knew I needed to hold back on the details a little. I was happy to let her know that I saw she got a room in my property; I would let her know I did it so I could keep an eye on her. So, I could keep her close. I would tell her that all those years she thought she was alone I was always there beside her waiting for the right time. Waiting for now.

Chapter 25

A.

Putting the phone back on the bedside table I looked over towards Tim. I wasn't sure whether to share what Lucy had just told me. We were desperate to move and carry on our life together somewhere Tim felt safe, but I didn't want to be indebted to Mathew Mason in any way. I must have stared too long as Tim caught my gaze.

"Penny for your thoughts."

"erm, that was Lucy, I texted her new year and asked her to ask her friend Eric if he knew of any properties going, she mentioned it to Mathew, and he has a few flats that have just been refurbed apparently."

He bounded over to the bed excitement on his face.

"that's brilliant Mandy, did she say where?"

"Erm yeah, Havering, Romford I think."

"Well, ring her then find out more, fuck it give me the phone I will ring her, is she with Matti boy now?"

He took the phone and hit call on Lucy's name. She answered quickly, from what I can make out a few happy new years were exchanged, and he asked to be passed onto Mathew. Listening to one side of the conversation I managed to get the gist of what was going on. Gesturing at me to get him a pen Tim wrote down what I assumed was the address,

"thanks, fella, and what's the postcode? RM3 hmm yep seven or eleven? Well I am definitely interested, and Mandy knows the area, we will see you there tomorrow at two, excellent thanks again mate."

Rm3 that was familiar leaning over to look over Tim's shoulder I was shocked to see the address. Tim put the phone down and beamed at me.

"Sounds good Mandy, what a start to the new year."

"Tim, I know that address."

"Brilliant what's the area like?"

"No, I mean I know it, I used to live there!"

"Really that's a bit strange! still, I have arranged to meet him tomorrow have a look around the place."

A bit strange! That was an understatement! I made my excuses and left the room not sure I could hide the emotions running through my head. That was my old house, Mathew owned the block! This was monumental, did he own it when I moved there? Of course, he did it was too much of a coincidence. Where did I get the details about the room? I couldn't recall? But sitting here now looking back it was becoming clear. Mathew had orchestrated it from the very beginning the job, the flat! Everything I had done to escape his memory was, in fact, me running into his lair. But why? Why would he dump me then move me into his house? I didn't understand. My resolution to steer clear of Mathew had suddenly become very complicated. I tried not to read too much into things and continued to enjoy the rest of our visit with my family.

I had made up with my mum last night and was worried things would feel uneasy, I had no grounds to worry the atmosphere between us was fantastic. I was pleased to see Tim was getting along with her, at one point he broke away to talk to me.

"I'm glad you didn't want me to choose between you and your mum baby, I'm not sure I would have chosen you, she is amazing."

I punched him in the arm

"Cheeky bastard, good job I love you and her for that matter!"

My mum cooked a beautiful meal at hers later that day, it was strange at first being back in there the place was unrecognisable, my mum loved to decorate it was her favourite past time, the living room had likely had ten different looks since I had left. The only original feature was the back door everything else looked different. Cleaner newer and fresher. I helped mum load the dishwasher and took a chance to thank her properly for dinner.

"Thanks for having us mum, we have had a lovely time."

"No problem darling I'm glad I could finally do it for you. It becomes a bit of a tradition having Livvy and the girls over New Year's Day. We always said a little word about you, you know just to remind each other how much we loved you."

Again, my tear ducts got the better of me as tears fell down my face.

"Thanks, mum it means so much to hear you say that."

"Oh, sweetheart don't cry come here."

With that I went to my mum, I didn't cry, nope I sobbed, I sobbed until my body shook years of unspent tears fell onto my poor mum's shoulders. At one point Tim stuck his head in the door saw us and patted my arm then slowly backed out knowing we needed to have this time together.

The session with my mum was therapeutic but draining I was exhausted as a result. All I wanted to do was curl up into a ball and sleep, but work resumed for me tomorrow, so I had to make my way back home. Hugging mum at the door, I promised to return in a couple of weeks, and hopefully, if all went well she could come to visit us once our move was sorted. Tim was in great spirits it was as though he tied all the previous negativity that had swamped us lately to our flat and the idea of moving so soon was the light at the end of the tunnel for him.

We went our separate ways at the station, Tim needed to get his bits from his mum. I didn't push too much, but I was pretty sure it was a stalling technic so he never had to spend the night in the flat, from what I could make out he had pinned his hopes on getting the keys from Mathew tomorrow and moving straight away.

"Your train says it's two minutes off Mandy, you better go to your platform."

"Okay I'm off, have a safe journey baby, and I will see you tomorrow?"

"Hmmm yep I will be home first thing then after you have been to work we can go to look at this flat in Romford, I have such a good feeling about it Mandy."

"I know you do baby, quick give me a kiss I can hear my train!"

Kissing my husband quickly I trotted down the stairs as my homebound train pulled into the station. I knew he was excited about going to view the Romford flat, but I was a lot more apprehensive. Something didn't feel right. It would be the first-time Mathew, Tim and myself had been in a room together since I had foolishly had sex with Mathew I was so nervous. I knew I had no choice I needed to go to see Mathew tonight. Clear the air and make sure my husband never found out about that night. Picking my phone up, I dropped Lucy a text. A pretence that I was seeing how her new year had gone gave me the information I was after.

She was spending the evening with her brothers. Mathew had been invited but said he had work to prepare for the morning. Safe in the knowledge he would be alone I started to think about what I would say to him. In short, I wanted to say, sorry we had sex please don't tell my husband, maybe that needed a bit of work, but hopefully, we could come to some kind of understanding.

M.

The London apartment offered fantastic views over the city, I was a little sad I never spent a new year here as the fireworks are always a spectacle. It was nippy out on the balcony the wind was whipping up a storm, passers-by were seen below, tiny dots holding onto hats and wayward umbrellas. Breathing in the cold winter air, I felt invincible. On top of the world almost literally being this high up was intoxicating. The buzzer interrupted my thoughts signalling the doorman wanting my attention. It was late but not too late that he was off duty. Assuming it was Lucy, I picked up the intercom.

"Mr Mason, Richard at reception speaking I have a guest to see you."

"Thank you, Richard; who is it please?"

"A young lady by the name of Mrs March."

It took a while for me to process that Mrs March was Amanda! What a pleasant surprise.

"Send her up please Richard."

I felt nervous, I shouldn't have done, this is what I wanted Amanda running to me in the middle of the night, but still I was unsure. I was also excited so incredibly excited my body was buzzing with anticipation. Her soft knock at the door signalled her arrival. I took a moment to appreciate how momentous this moment was. Looking at her through the spy hole burning the image into my brain. Today was the day my life would truly change, and I was more than ready. Opening the door, I ushered her in.

"Amanda, it's so good to see you I have missed you!"

I had, so much so that it had hurt, seeing her here now in my lobby I felt whole, it was as though I had lived with a hole in my chest my entire life and having her back with me had healed that void. She looked at me a little hesitantly.

"Hello Mathew"

Moving towards her for an embrace I was surprised when she stepped out of my grasp. Maybe I was jumping the gun a little, whilst I knew it was time for us to be together Amanda had yet to be privy to the information. I took her hand in mine. Amanda, please don't shun me this is right, you and I, we are meant to be together there is little point in fighting it. I'm tired of behaving distantly around you tired of pretending you're unimportant, you're so significant to me Amanda, sometimes I think you're the only reason I wake up each morning. Let's just give in to this now Amanda,

"Let's just be together."

Her face did not display the emotions I would have expected instead she looked a little confused.

"Mathew, I'm sorry as you know I'm married. What you're saying is very sudden. I don't know what to say how to react. I love Tim very much, I came to talk to you to see if we could bury what happened between us. It would destroy Tim if he found out."

"Don't you see what I'm saying, Amanda? Forget him I'm here now, I am claiming you. You wouldn't want for anything; I will support you and care for you. Tim was a glitch, I'm the real deal."

Once again confusion etched across her face and then she laughed! I was offering her the world and the scrawny little bitch laughed. I was not the type of man to be laughed at!

"I'm sorry Mathew I think you have your wires crossed. I am not here to start anything with you I'm here to end things to make it clear the other week was a mistake."

I was startled by her response, this was not what I had expected from her, how could she not feel what I felt? My resolve to be nice crumbled much quicker than I would have liked. Taking a large step towards her, I pushed her frail body against the wall. Kissing at her mouth, she did not respond I move my trail of kisses down her neck

"Mathew please we can't."

She pushed at me, but I was so much stronger than her I didn't move, lowering my hand to her waistband she let out a startled cry

"Please Mathew no, I love my husband I won't do this, get off me."

My hand slipped into her waistband without effort.

"Amanda, does Tim know our history?"

She shook her head as a response.

"So let me get this straight, you keep our past a secret from your husband, yet you come to me late at night. How do you think he would feel if he heard about that Amanda. If he heard how you threw yourself at me not only when you were a young girl, and I was a happily married man but a few weeks ago then again tonight? , Coming to my apartment begging me to fuck you, your tiny tight little body begging me to take you right here in my hallway?"

She let out a small whimper as I pushed my hand between her legs, taking my time I slowly inserted my finger, she was tight and resistant.

"He won't like it Amanda will he, so here's what's going to happen, you are going to let me do what I want to you tonight, and I won't tell him."

Any resolve I had made to woo Amanda was dissolving fast. How quickly I had changed back to the bad Mathew the one Amanda only knew in her sleep, the Mathew that took what he wanted from her when he wanted. I had shown her my true colours now, and although she didn't want to, she let me take her right there. I explored her body like never before taking her every way I have dreamed of, no longer conscious of hurting or marking her, I punished her for all the years she had been away. Her initial protest and cries only spurring me on more, for tonight she was mine. We settled into a strange routine, I would abuse her body how I saw fit them comfort her as she silently wept, only the tears would spur me on again her sorrow being my aphrodisiac. This went on all night hour after hour; it was as though she was on drug. My body had no choice but to react to her, the sun rose over my shoulder yet my stamina never faltered, her demeanour never altered. She was quiet and absent refusing to meet my eye giving her body over to me to do with as I see fit. Eventually, I had enough, my body was sore and my mind quiet. I fell, exhausted and sedate next to her. "Thank- you Amanda, that was amazing" For the first time since I had started touching her she met my eye.

"Why Mathew?"

I had only one answer

"Because you are mine!

"I'm not yours Mathew I could have been many years ago, for years I waited for you, looked out for you in a crowd Hoped you would come for me, but you left me, Mathew, what just happened, that was not okay do you understand that?"

"I never left you, Amanda, I was always there, always with you. I was with you before you met me. Your life embroiders with mine. I owned you before you even knew my name."

She shook her head

"I don't understand why are you talking in riddles, what's going on?"

Cupping her face in my hand, I began to tell her our story,

"Amanda my beautiful delicate, damaged girl, you don't know much about me, so I'm going to fill you in. I'm a bad man Amanda, I seek the company of young girls to get my kicks and thrills. I know it is wrong and know it's bad but it's part of me, embedded in my very being. I first saw you maybe fifteen years ago, you were at who I now know to be your sisters, you caught my eye as many young girls before you have. I saw you again at greens the shopping Centre, it's long ago been demolished, do you remember it?"

She nodded in response a look of horror on her face. Wiping a stray tear from her eye.

"Don't be upset Amanda it's wasted I can't benefit from your sorrow at the moment I'm truly spent, I followed you back from the shopping Centre Amanda, I have to admit I became a little obsessed. I needed to have you at all costs. So I did, I waited one evening till your mother went out and snuck into your room; you were drugged and unconscious. I took your beautiful body, and it sparked a lifetime's obsession, the problem is Amanda, you affected me like no other, you soothed me; I was never happier purer or more human than when I was immersed in you.

I'm afraid you may have been hurt over the years, I was sorry to read I had impregnated you that night it was not my intention."

Amanda's face was drained of all colour she sat listening to me the look of disbelief on her face,"

"What night, what do you mean read?"

"The night we first met Amanda when you were fifteen, as for reading, your little diary's, did you really believe I couldn't see them? Your little trials and tribulations of a troubled typist. You have no idea how much time I have invested in you Amanda, the time I spent sculpturing you to perfection. No idea how much I have had to sacrifice to keep in the shadows. I had convinced myself that once I had you in the purest form, I wouldn't need you anymore but you were woven into my being. Something neither of us could change. So, I invented a job for you, so I could spend more time with you up close and personal. At seventeen you were maybe a little too old for my tastes but it stopped being about your age and was more about you, it was you I sought out you I needed. Fifteen years of living in your shadows having to be content to breathe in your sheets or watch you from afar, I saved you on a few occasions, Amanda, saved you from people that wanted to hurt you, Nate for example, he was not good for you, he had to go."

She began to reach next to me her stomach seemingly too weak for some of our truths. Perhaps I had been too honest, perhaps I should have sedated her and let her wake none the wiser, but I was so tired, so tired of the game and of the fight, she needed to know the truth. Her rejection had surprised me maybe I had been delusional assuming she would want me as much as I would want her, to assume she would need me too, I did need her she was my vice, and now I needed her to help cleanse my soul one last time. Nobody is born a victim Amanda, but they are made. It seems I may have made you my victim."

Her voice was weak and sorrowful I had to strain to hear her

"Why Mathew?"

"Have you ever truly needed someone, Amanda? Needed them so much it stopped you making rational decisions. Have you ever needed to be so close to someone that being inside them isn't enough? You need to own them to control them? I don't suppose you have. But when you're a person like me loving them and holding them isn't enough. To submit to them feelings made me weak, my father taught me one thing Amanda, never let your heart rule your head, at times I stepped a fine line, for so long I kept my distance. It's only now I realise that the times I did cross the line when I used your body to silence my chaotic mind it was them times when I found peace it was at that time I was in my purest form, and it was then that I loved you."

The words shocked me, but I knew them to be true. I loved her more than I could ever have anticipated. First, she broke my heart and now she was breaking my spirit.

"It's a lot for you to take on Amanda, hush now I think you should sleep."

Carrying her broken body to my bed I lie her down, going to my bathroom cabinet to retrieve a sedative. I see movement out of the corner of my eye. She was attempting to run I caught her easily, and her body slumped against mine in defeat.

"Shush don't cry my sweet, you are going to go to sleep and tomorrow I will let you go back home to your husband if you wish, do you want that Amanda."

I think a piece of me broke when she nodded I was still hoping after all I had told her she would choose me, administering the sedative I watched sleep take her.

The calm was broken by the shrill of my phone ringing, picking up the phone I see it was already eleven AM, how time fly's when you're having fun, checking the screen, I let it go to voice mail.

Retrieving the message I heard Lucy's nasally voice

"Mathew It's me, Lucy, listen I'm confused I don't understand what's going on. Amanda is missing I have had Tim on the phone, she didn't make it home last night and hasn't come into work this morning. Tim mentioned something about you and Amanda?"

Her voice cracked as she began to cry,

"Mathew I don't understand, Tim rang Amanda's mum looking for her, they somehow got to discussing you? They must have been discussing the new flat, her mum knows of you like I said I don't understand, apparently you two have a history she was once expecting your child? Mathew? Mathew, are you there? Please? Tim is on his way over to you now. I'm hoping he has it all wrong ring me once you get this message, please."

Looking at my beautiful Amanda, I made my way to her. Lying upon her beautiful, frail body, I allowed myself to enjoy her edges and bones so beautiful so fragile. Placing my hands around her neck I gripped tight, she did not protest she did not fight she just submitted to me, submitted to my will the way I had always desired.

Watching her failing body take her last breaths I felt my stone heartbreak. I haven't cried in forty years yet sitting in my bedroom watching her life ebb away the tears flowed. She was my mother, my sister, my lover and my child all rolled into one, and now she was gone, I no longer had anything to live for. I lay with her body until it began to cool. The urge came again, and I enjoyed her flesh once more. She had never been more beautiful, more still or more angelic. The intercom to my apartment buzzed into life. Leaving her body on the bed, I move towards the balcony. My soul was cleansed and my mind quiet. The wind was strong; it was difficult to open the balcony door. Climbing onto the railing, my skin Prickled at the cold, standing on the edge naked and pure I stretched my arms out to my side, as I leant into the wind for a moment I hovered, the wind suspending me mid-air. Then I fell.

THE END

If your enjoyed Sculpting Amanda, please follow the author at
http://www.facebook.com/juliesanfordauthor/

New material, coming soon.

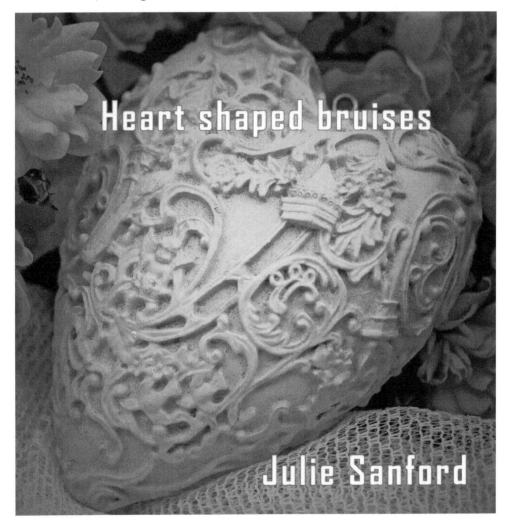

Allow me to introduce myself, I am Olivia but occasionally I use the name Melissa. I am a mature student, a trainee teacher, plus a mum to my two beautiful girls.

My useless husband managed to get himself locked up at her majesties pleasure. This means the girls upbringing has been left to me.

It's a struggle, times are hard and moneys tight. Fortunately, I have found a way to make money, it's not conventional but it works for me. Occasionally, under the cover of darkness I attend adult parties. Whilst there I like to share my body with strangers.

Does that make me a bad person?

I don't think so; can I confess something? I am more worried how bad I would become if I never done it.

Printed in Great Britain
by Amazon